SINFUL DISTRACTION

A TEMPERANCE FALLS ROMANCE

LONDON HALE

SINFUL *distraction*

LONDON HALE

LONDON HALE

Dedicated to all the women still fighting like hell to break those glass ceilings.

chapter one

RILEY

IF ANYONE HAD told me a year ago that watching a meeting of the Temperance Falls town council on the public access channel would get me hard, I'd have laughed in their face. One phone call, one life-changing move, and I wasn't laughing anymore. But I *was* hard. Hard enough to wish I could tear my eyes away from the screen and go rub one out. I didn't want to miss a second of this, though.

On the television, the mayor of Temperance Falls stood at a podium in the council room. Her blond hair hung straight, not quite touching her slim shoulders, and she had her glasses on. The same ones that featured in just about every fantasy I had.

"The proposed mixed-use facility would offer inexpensive housing options for residents, office space for small businesses, and a retail base that can bring more revenue to the island, while supplying much-needed jobs in our community."

Fuck, the woman was hot when she got all naughty-professor. She was also way more than just her looks. She was strong and sure, completely in command of the room. She spoke to the people sitting around her with a confidence I practically panted for. The woman was a rock star in the local political scene because of her beauty, but her mind was the real gem. That and her always-in-control attitude drew me to her. Well, and her sexy-as-fuck voice. It all came down to her voice.

Some stuffy old guy in a tweed sport coat to her right leaned forward, grabbing the mic in front of him. "From the plans provided, the population density in that area will quadruple. The island itself will increase at least fifteen percent. Do you really think our infrastructure can handle that?"

Oh yeah, her infrastructures could handle anything. I snuck in a cock adjustment as Kate seemed to take a moment to collect her thoughts. Here it came—the moment I'd been waiting for. Assertive Kate was about to shift to Aggressive Kate. My girl was going to tear his ass apart, and I was likely about to come in my sweats listening to her do it.

"Councilman Nicholson, as I included in the project guidelines before you, the current infrastructure can support a partial filling of the space. That said, I believe we can scale our services with the population growth of the project. The mixed-use facility will bring more people, sure, but it will also bring more tax revenue. At only seventy-percent capacity, it will bring three times the tax revenue we received when the mall was open and filled. That population means more first responders needed, and that tax revenue will supply the funds to acquire them. Furthermore…"

Man, I loved it when she furthermored. If I were in my apartment alone, I'd be jacking my cock already. Hell, I'd have been halfway to coming the second she took the podium. Too bad I didn't have cable in my little place over the garage. I had to hang out at my parents' house to watch Kate do her thing. Soon enough, I'd get to watch it in person.

"Why are you watching this crap, Riley? Since when do you care what the town council is doing?" Claire, my sister and a permanent pain in my ass, plopped onto the couch beside me, staring at the television with a frown. Luckily for me, she was also a hard-on killer. One problem solved.

"I don't…usually." Totally not a lie. The council didn't matter; Kate did. But I wouldn't tell Claire that. "I'm a city employee now, sis. I need to keep an eye on the council to see if things affect the department, that's all."

She huffed, shaking her head. "One brother's a cop, the other's a fireman who also works construction on his days off. We're a walking, talking Irish-American stereotype."

"We don't have red hair."

"Your beard is looking a little red."

I ran a hand over my chin. Yeah, it did, which

was why I usually shaved every day. I'd been busy that morning at the firehouse, though. By the time I'd gotten off—four hours past my scheduled leave time—I'd been too tired from my shift to do more than take a quick shower and rush to my parents' living room to watch the council meeting.

The firehouse schedule of forty-eight hours on and forty-eight off fit my life pretty well at the moment. I accumulated a lot of overtime because of the fact that I had neither a wife nor kids to get home to, plus I picked up odd jobs over at the old lighthouse revitalization project on my off days. All that meant I worked a lot of fucking hours. Sometimes, shaving just didn't take priority outside of the firehouse. Had to keep clean shaven for the breathing masks.

The old man—Nicholson, Kate had called him— had asked another question, one I'd missed, and Kate's polished veneer was starting to show signs of wear. Her normally calm, slightly fake smile had dropped, her lips a sliver away from frowning, and her placid eyes were filling with a fire I could spot even through the grainy footage on the television fifteen feet away. She looked ready to snap, but there was nothing I could do. No way I could shore her up when she needed someone to. Shit.

C'mon, Kitten. Use your claws.

"Councilman Nicholson, while I understand your concerns, I think we need to take the risk if we want Temperance Falls to remain the vibrant community it is today. That's an eighty-acre superblock site with a 200,000 square-foot building sitting empty and rotting. The entire mass-market area on that side of the island is suffering because of it, as are home prices. Residents want something in that space. The building is a liability right now. I'd like to make it an asset, and Huntley Group wants to invest almost a billion dollars to make that a reality."

Claws…Kate definitely had them. Fuck, she was ridiculous when she went all badass professional. How did every man in that room not have a hard-on for her?

"Seriously, why are we watching this?" Claire grabbed the remote and pointed it at the television.

I had my arm banded across her and my hand over hers before she could press the buttons. "Don't change it."

"Why?" She struggled under my hold, shoving at me with both hands. "I don't want to watch this."

The girl could wrestle, that was for sure. Growing up with two older brothers had probably helped that skill along. Ow, when did she learn to twist my arm like that?

"Too bad." Still reaching for the remote, I grunted as her foot connected with my gut. Damn, she was strong.

"Can you two cut it out?" Mom hurried across the room, carrying a basket of laundry. "I swear, you both act like children. Why can't you be more like your brother?"

Claire stopped fighting, giving me one more shove to push me off her. I sat up, rolling my eyes as Claire did the same, both of us mouthing *fucking*

Connor as my mom left the room. It was hard being the younger siblings of a golden child. I was the flighty one, the drifter. The one who'd left the house right after graduation and moved off the island. Claire was the baby and would probably always be seen as such. But Connor? He was the savior. The policeman. The one who never did anything wrong. I would have bet money his life was boring as shit, but what did I know?

I'd been gone for years, only having moved back recently to join the firehouse and get my life together. I was done with drifting. One call from Kate—one year of increasingly frequent calls, in fact—had set that plan in motion in my mind. Move home, get a good job, kick-start a life that was worth her attention. I was almost there, too. Almost ready. Just a few more months, and I could make my move.

By the time I looked back at the television, Kate was gone from behind the podium, and the council had moved on to other business.

"Shit." I dropped back into my seat. "I wanted to watch that."

Claire huffed, still looking irritated with me. "I'll never understand why."

I shrugged, wishing she knew my reasoning. Wishing I could tell her, my mom, my brother—the whole world, really—that I was in love with Mayor Kate Briscoe. But I couldn't. Hell, I couldn't even tell Kate that. Not yet. She didn't exactly know who I was.

Before I could say anything else, my phone rang.

I glanced at the screen, expecting to ignore the caller, but the number made me jump up.

"I have to take this." I was across the room and out the door in seconds, hurrying toward the privacy of the apartment over the garage as I swiped my screen to accept the call. "I didn't expect to hear from you today."

The woman on the other end—the boss of what I would call my side job—chuckled. "She's calling for you."

"I figured since she's the only calls I take."

"Should I put her through?"

I shoved open the door and let it slam behind me, pausing only long enough to lock it. I did *not* want to be interrupted. "Absolutely."

"Give me five, sugar." My boss disappeared, leaving me with nothing but silence on the line.

I kept the phone to my ear as I stripped off my sweats and tossed them across the room. The same room that had been mine during my senior year in high school. I hadn't ever expected to live here again, to bring my life back to Temperance Falls, and especially not to live over the garage at my childhood home once more. I'd run as soon as I'd gotten out of school, had headed to the mainland to start a life. I'd been a bartender, a waiter, had worked in retail and offices, been a balloon-animal maker and a carnival ride jockey…but it wasn't until I'd gotten a job working on the phones that I'd found something I liked to do.

No career day bullshit had prepared me to be a

phone sex operator, but it was a damn good job. I made bank talking to women—and sometimes men—from all across the country. Well, *mostly* talking. Sometimes things got heated. Sometimes, they got damn well steamy. The first call I'd received from Kate? That had been downright sex with words. Luckily, she'd called again. And then another time, always asking for me. Always giving me little glimpses into her world as we talked about life, about our frustrations, and about how wet her pussy would be if I got my tongue on it. I'd fallen in love with her over the phone.

Too bad she had no idea who I really was, or that I'd moved home just to be close to her.

I was completely naked, lying on my bed with my hand already around the base of my cock, when I finally heard her breathing come across the line. I knew how this would go. She'd wait for me to say something, give up her assertive personality to be the timid one between us. I played along because it was what she needed, but I looked forward to the day when she took control with me. I ached for it.

"Hey there, Kitten. This is a surprise."

Fuck, her breathy sigh made me want to strip her down and find out what else I could do to get her to make that sound. What parts of her body I could tease with my fingers and tongue to elicit such an adorable response.

"I know it's not our usual day—" she started, but I cut that shit off quick.

"You can call me anytime. You know that."

"I do," she said, and the telltale rustle of fabric

told me she was probably still in her suit. The one I'd seen her in just fifteen minutes ago on the television. "It's been a rough day, and I needed to hear your voice."

I let my fingers run along the length of my cock, dreaming of what it would feel like if they were hers. I wanted that so much, wanted to know if she'd be gentle or demanding. Would she stroke me from the base to the tip, play more with the head? Would she take me in her mouth and swallow me down as I came? I sure as hell hoped so, and I couldn't wait until the day I found out.

"So," I asked, ready to play the role. Ready to give her what she needed. "How was your day?"

Her groan was expected, as was her tired response. "Brutal. Thank God I wore my nude shoes today because I had to stand a lot. My legs are killing me."

Yeah, she'd had to stand behind that podium arguing with the council. My Kate loved her heels, but they wreaked havoc on her sometimes. Especially the pink ones. I had no idea what the pink ones looked like, but I was going to burn those fuckers one day. They caused her too much pain.

"If I were there, I'd rub those long legs for you. I'd run you a bubble bath first, though. Maybe get you a glass of wine. I'd always have your favorite ready because you work so damn hard."

"I know you would," she said, her voice growing softer. Warmer. She loved this script.

"And when you were all warm and relaxed—and maybe a little tipsy—I'd lay you on the bed and rub my hands all over you. Rub out any knot. Would you like that? You think me touching every single inch of you would help you relax?"

"God, yes, Banner."

Aaaannnnddddd…bingo. She was ready. Her voice always took on that moany edge when she was aroused. Just a couple months more, and I'd hear it in person. Hell, I'd get to hear that voice saying my real name. I couldn't fucking wait. But for now, she needed me to play a part for her, and I was damn good at my job. "What can I do tonight? What do you need from me to make it all better?"

She was silent for a long minute, long enough that I began to wonder if I'd missed something big at the council meeting. Long enough that I worried something else was up. But finally, she sighed.

"I need you, Banner." Her voice had dropped, her words going slightly breathy. Her close voice. Her fully-into-the moment voice. Yeah, she needed me, all right. Needed me in the same way I'd been needing her since I first saw her walk into that meeting earlier tonight.

"I'm always here for you," I said, easing up on my phone-sex voice. The one I used to wind her up. The one my boss called "the panty-melter" voice. Kate knew it as the voice of Banner, the man she called when she needed a release. The man she paid weekly to have phone sex with her.

"I need your words," she whispered, sounding altogether aroused. "I just want to let go. I want to come with you tonight. I need it."

I tightened my grip on my cock, trying not to

blow right then. "Oh, Kitten. You know I can give you that. I'd give you anything, sweet girl. So tell me…how quick can you be naked and sprawled out on your bed for me? I've got all the time in the world for you, and I think I need to pay some close, personal attention to your pretty pussy tonight."

chapter two

KATE

BANNER'S WORDS SETTLED over me, the smooth cadence of his voice something my body had begun to recognize months ago. My limbs went loose and languid, my nipples tightening, even my pussy grew warm. Just from his *voice*. Whenever I heard that decadent sound, it meant release was imminent. It meant my time as Mayor Briscoe was put on hold. Whatever deals were in the pipeline, whatever political bullshit I had to manage, whatever jackass councilman currently trying to get in my way were all shoved aside. My time as just Kate—or Kitten to Banner—was about to start.

There were never any pretenses between us. I didn't have to put on a show, didn't have to wear my mask—the mask every professional woman had to wear. The one that said *I got here by working hard, and*

I will take zero percent of your shit. But the part I loved the most was that I could let go of all that control, all that power I had to cling to day in and day out to do my job well. To *prove* I could do that job just as well— better—than any man in the same position. I could give up that control over the safety of the phone and not worry what it said about me that I didn't want to think for a little while. That I *liked* when Banner told me exactly what to do, exactly how to do it, and for exactly how long.

"C'mon, baby. Strip for me. I want you naked so I can give you what you need."

I nearly melted as his voice came over the line, but I did as he instructed. I always did. "I am…slowly. Just how you like."

He groaned, the sound shooting straight to my pussy. This…*this* was my reward for putting in sixty-plus hours at city hall, these thirty minutes the only ones during my week when I didn't have to think, and I relished every single one of them. Loved hearing his voice. Craved it on the days we didn't talk.

Like today. We *never* talked on Tuesdays. I almost hadn't called, worried he wouldn't be available—or worse, that he wouldn't take my call at all since it wasn't the norm. We did Friday evenings at nine like clockwork.

It'd been like that for nearly a year—since the first day my friend Lara had slipped this number into my hand and told me I needed to do something about all the tension I was carrying. In her words, I needed to get laid, and I needed to get laid hard. Since she knew the men on the island didn't do it for me—not to mention the fact that the mayor couldn't exactly get her rocks off in a commitment-free arrangement— she'd suggested the next best thing, a company that provided a service she thought might be a good fit for me.

"I hear the rustle of your clothes coming off. Fuck, I wish I were there to see the show, watch you strip nice and slow. I'd make you tease me with every inch of your skin while I stroked my cock. No one could ever make me as hard as you do. I'd be so fucking lucky to get even a glimpse of your body."

And, Jesus, how could a flesh and blood man compete with *that*? They couldn't. Even if the Temperance Falls gossip mill weren't pumping full time with every little thing each resident did— never mind the mayor—I wasn't sure I'd want an arrangement, commitment-free or not. Been there, done that. If there was a man out there with enough confidence to handle a powerful woman navigating a demanding career, doing absolutely fine on her own, I hadn't yet found him. And I was damn tired of looking. Actually, I'd passed damn tired of looking more than a decade ago.

Thank God I had Banner to call so I could unwind and go to sleep sated and relaxed. After a day like I'd had—one where being a high-powered woman made me a target for every small-dicked asshole hell-bent on making my life shit—it would've been nice to come home to a comforting face, to a hard body ready to work away every ounce of stress I had. Would've been *nice,* but not at the expense of myself or the career for which I'd worked my ass off.

Instead, I had my phone, Banner's voice, and whatever he guided me to do. It wasn't perfect, but it worked for me. And it was the most intimate relationship I'd had with a man in, well, ever. What did that say about me?

"Where'd you go, Kitten?"

I settled onto my bed, blowing out a breath. "Sorry, I'm here. Just have a lot on my mind."

"Is everything okay?" he asked, his voice laced with concern.

I didn't know if this was part of the act—part of being *Banner* instead of whatever he went by in his real life—but if it was, he was a damn good actor. From the very beginning, his reactions had seemed authentic—his arousal, his happiness, his concern, even his anger when I'd mentioned any of the hundreds of piles of bullshit I dealt with on a weekly basis. He was always with me, every step of the way.

It made me feel like we had more of a connection than two unknown people getting off together over the phone.

Regardless of that connection—imagined or not—I couldn't give him details. Couldn't tell him Nicholson was doing everything in his power to stop me at every turn where Huntley Group was concerned. Couldn't tell him anything that would give a clue of who I was.

I brushed a piece of hair away from my face. "It's just been an exceptionally exhausting day."

"So that's why the Tuesday night love. You couldn't wait for Friday."

Actually, it was a wonder I could wait for Friday every week. If I'd managed it after this shitshow of a week, it would've been a damn miracle. "Yeah. Did it mess up your schedule?"

"You could never mess up anything."

I hummed, wanting desperately to believe his words but at the same time knowing with certainty he told all his clients that.

"Now tell me," he said, rustling coming over the line. I imagined he was in bed, settled against dark sheets, his large hand wrapped around his even larger cock. Stroking. Teasing. He wasn't even with me, and he could make me shudder more than half the men I'd been with. "What do you really need from me right now? What is it that I can do to make your shitty day better?"

Relaxing back into the pillows, I closed my eyes and focused on the image behind my lids. I could never see a clear picture of his face in these daydreams, no matter how hard I tried. His body was ripped, his muscles a force of nature—an image I'd concocted thanks to something he'd mentioned during one of our early calls. The name he went by was an ode to what his friends called him during high school: Hulk. Since Hulk didn't exactly exude sexiness, he'd settled on Banner, as in Dr. Bruce Banner. He'd said his stature was something that intimidated some people, but not me. If he were in front of me, I'd rub my hands over every inch of him, relishing in his size.

Strangely, though, that wasn't even what I focused on during these sessions. It was more the overall *feeling* of being with him, his voice directly in my ear washing over me, relaxing me… The connection we'd formed was incredibly intimate.

Trailing a finger between my breasts, I answered his question. "I want you to do the same thing you always do. I need your words so I can stop thinking."

"I think you need more than words. I think you need my hands on you."

Like his very suggestion held magic, the image of him on a strange bed faded, and suddenly he was in my bedroom, his fingers ghosting over me. "I wish I could have your hands on me."

He paused for so long I worried the call had dropped, but then he swore under his breath. "I wish for that too. You have no idea. Now, are you naked for me?"

"Mhmm, I'm on my bed and ready. Unless you want me to get a toy—"

"Tonight's about what you need. If you want a toy, I'll make you believe it's my cock. If not, we can get more creative. What do you need from me? What part of me will make you wet tonight?"

Dozens of fantasies flipped through my mind as I tried to settle on one of the many different scenarios we'd acted out over the phone. As much as I wanted his cock, wanted to be filled by him, I knew a dildo would be a poor substitute, and not having him in reality would only make me feel lonelier. "Your mouth. I want your mouth."

He groaned, as if the very thought of his lips on me pushed him closer to the edge. "Get that toy you bought, Kitten. The one you said sucks on your clit. That's what I'd do. Once I licked you all over and got you good and swollen, I'd suck that clit until you were riding my face. I'd want to be under you when you came. Would want to taste every drop. Get the toy, and let's play."

I shuddered out a breath, halfway to coming just from his dirty mouth, and reached into my bedside table for my favorite toy. Resting the phone between my shoulder and my ear, I parted my pussy with a hand, exposing my clit, then turned on the toy to the lowest setting and placed the silicone head directly over my clit. "I've got—" A moan poured from my lips, and my eyes fluttered closed when I bumped the speed up a notch, the isolated suction as close to oral as I could get.

He chuckled, low and deep. "I know you love that one. I figure I've got three minutes before that toy gets you off, right? I remember the first time. You came so hard you dropped the phone."

I breathed out a laugh, recalling the day he was talking about. I'd had no idea what I'd been in for, but sweet Jesus, it'd been as close as the two of us could ever get to him going down on me. I loved it for that intimacy alone. "I don't know if I can come that fast tonight. It's been—" I broke off, a shiver running through my body as the toy did exactly what it promised, working me up just like someone sucking on my clit. "It's been a long day."

"If I were there, I'd get you to come right away to take the edge off. I'd catch you as you walked in the door and push up that little pencil skirt I know you wear to the office. I'd have those panties down and my mouth on you before I even said hello. A good woman deserves a man who'll treat her like a princess when she needs it. My princess likes to get her clit sucked, doesn't she? She likes the idea of me sliding my tongue into her pussy, too. Is that what you need right now, baby?"

"God, yes," I said on a moan, no longer able to keep my eyes open.

"I've got you. You feel that pressure on your clit? Feel how it's making you so wet? That's me. All me. I'd lap up every drop, suckle you until you screamed my name. Spread your legs for me. I need room to work that pussy and make you come. My hands would be on your thighs right now, pushing your knees down to open you wide. Such a pretty view for me. Are you dripping yet? Do you need my fingers?"

My nipples drew tight, the points nearly painful in their hardness. I was on the precipice, certain a breeze could make me go off. But still, I held out. I drew out the buildup as long as I could, because I knew once I came, our time would be over. I wasn't ready for that yet. "Yes, I need—please, Banner, I need—"

"I know what you need. Bump that toy up another level for me. That's what I'd do—I'd be sucking so hard on you. Are your legs shaking yet? Your thighs always tremble just before you come. That's when I'd slip three fingers inside you. Not one or two—no, my Kitten's a greedy girl. She needs three. Needs a good hard thrust inside to fill her up. Don't you? Slide your fingers inside yourself and pretend they're mine."

Switching my phone to speaker, I set it on my stomach so I could do what he instructed. I slid my fingers down to my pussy, stroking around the toy suctioned onto my clit, before slipping them inside, groaning at how wet I was. I wished it were him doing that, wished it were his fingers filling me up, wished it were his tongue lapping at my clit instead of a toy. But I had his voice. Right then, I had his voice and his words and his commands, and for a short while, I didn't have to think. Somehow, he knew exactly what I needed.

"Oh God…"

"Goddamn, you sound so wet. I can hear you. C'mon, just a little more. I can tell. You're breathing so hard, and you're making those little moans. I bet you're fucking dripping for me. I bet your legs are trembling all over. Fuck your hand. Rock those hips against it. I want to feel you come on my lips now. I want to hear you. Give it to me. Bump that toy up one last time and let go for me."

"I'm close—" I moaned, rocking against my hand just like he said, the toy sucking my clit. So close. So close… But I needed him with me. Whether it was real or not, I needed to pretend it was. "I want you to come with me."

"Fuck." He groaned. "Your hand would feel so good on my cock right now. Mmm, it does. I'm fucking my hand just like I'd fuck yours. Wish it was yours, baby. I always wish it was yours." His breath came in sharp pants, the rhythmic sound of him stroking his cock loud even through the phone. "Damn. I can hear you fucking your hand. All those filthy sucking sounds coming over the line. I love it. You sound ready. I'm so close—I'm going to come all over my hand in a second. Let me hear you first. Come on my tongue. Soak me, Kitten."

It was the hitch of his breath that did it as he said *Kitten*—something he couldn't fake, no matter how good of an actor he was. I pictured him in my bed, his face buried between my legs, his tongue hard at work on my clit, his fingers thrusting inside me. And his other hand wrapped around his cock, jerking it because he couldn't wait. Because licking me got him so worked up, he didn't have a choice but to fist his cock and stroke it as I came.

And I did.

Back arched off the bed, fingers buried deep, I came with his name on my lips, my hips shifting as if it were his face I was rocking them against.

"Christ. You came all over my mouth, didn't you? Love the taste of your sweetness. Want it, want it so bad—" A string of curses left his lips just before he moaned, long and deep, the sound so sexy it made me ache all over again.

I shut off my toy as I tried to catch my breath, listening as he did the same. Taking my phone off speaker, I pressed it to my ear once more, waiting for his words.

"Fuck, Kitten, you get me off so good. I haven't come that hard since Friday."

The last time we talked.

I smiled, even if what he said wasn't true. I appreciated the sentiment, nonetheless. "Me too. Thank you for that."

"You feeling better now?"

I blocked out the events of the day, refusing to let them intrude on our time. "I am. I'll hopefully be able to get some sleep tonight."

"Good, I'm glad I could help." He cleared his throat. "Is this our call for the week, or can I expect you again on Friday?"

The thought of waiting until the following Friday, of not speaking to him for nearly two weeks, opened up a cavern in my stomach. "I thought we could still do Friday, if that's okay. My schedule this week is going to be…" Hell. It was going to be hell. "A challenge."

"Of course it's okay. I wouldn't know what to do if we missed a Friday night." He sighed deeply, the sound of a man spent and exhausted. "Did you double-check your locks for me?"

I breathed out a laugh, rolling my eyes. I was forty-two, had lived on my own for two decades. I could handle locking my doors. Still, I couldn't help the warmth that settled over me when he reminded me of this. And he did—every time we talked. "Yes, they're all locked."

"All right, sweet girl. Try to get some sleep. I'll talk to you on Friday."

"Bye, Banner."

"Bye, Kitten."

I hung up the phone, an overwhelming sense of loneliness washing over me. The feeling settled in and didn't leave as I washed up for the evening, as I drank a glass of wine and went over my calendar for tomorrow. It didn't leave as I walked through my huge, empty house, as I triple-checked that the doors and windows were all locked.

And it certainly didn't leave as I slipped under the covers on my side of the king-size bed, Banner's voice in my memory my only companion.

chapter three

RILEY

FRIDAY HAD ALWAYS been my favorite day of the week. When I was a kid, it was because I couldn't wait to get two days away from school. When I grew older, even though I often worked weekends, Friday represented a time to hang out with friends and find the best party we could. For the past year, Friday meant spending half an hour or so with Kate. I might have even skipped out of the fire station like a fucking kid at the thought.

"Yo, Nash."

Damn. I'd been so intent on getting home that I hadn't noticed Big John rolling up beside me in his pickup. "What's up?"

"Me and a couple of guys are headed over to the Beerhive tonight. You should meet us." John's light eyes held mine, his Semper Fi baseball cap shading the top half of his face. He was the son of one of my mom's best friends, so we'd known each other a long time even if we were just getting reacquainted through our jobs as firemen. I'd left the island right after high school to escape—he'd left to join the Marines. Neither of us had been back for all that long.

We'd never hung out outside of work, though. Of course, I didn't hang out with a lot of the guys from the firehouse—most were married with kids. With lives. John wasn't married and didn't talk about a woman, so everyone else assumed he was single. I wasn't married and didn't talk about a woman either, so I assumed nothing. John could have his own Kate somewhere for all I knew.

"I would, man, but Friday nights are always booked." I almost left it at that, but I actually would've liked hanging out had it been any other day. Might as well build bridges in town. "Rain check, though."

John smiled and nodded, gripping the steering wheel. "For any night other than Friday. Got it. See you in two, bro. Make 'em count."

With that, he took off, some sort of seventies hard rock screaming through the windows. The man was right. I had forty-eight hours off, and I needed to make the next two days count. Kate tonight, apartment hunting tomorrow. I had work to do.

Instead of going straight home, I headed over to Main Street and down the line of shops. With Temperance Falls being a tourist town, there wasn't much on the strip that interested me. In fact, there was only one shop I had my eye on. Bundt and

Grind, the local coffeehouse. The place served a mean Americano, and the barista this time of day gave me an extra shot for free, plus they had these little cookie things I couldn't get enough of.

But the moment I walked in, instead of coffee or sweets or anything I'd expected to focus on, all I could see was her. Kate. She owned the room without trying to, eclipsing everything else with her very presence. A presence I was wholly unprepared for.

My body froze on the spot, my eyes going wide as they took in every detail. Kate sat at a bistro table near the front window, a folder in front of her. Her dark jacket made her hair stand out like a halo, and the peek of bright pink at her collar made me wonder what else on her would be pink. Long legs—bare, of course—crossed at the ankles, some sort of pink spiky shoes on her feet. A strong, confident businesswoman. But I knew her, knew she wore the color around her neck to soften her harshness. Knew that underneath her suit coat would be something silky or lacy. I knew those shoes on her feet were likely the pink ones she hated to love so much, and she'd complain about them later. I knew what she sounded like when she was fucking herself with a toy because I told her to. Hell, I knew I could get her off in fifteen minutes flat with just the right words if need be.

I knew that woman, but we'd never actually met.

My cock ached fiercely behind my zipper, pressing against the fabric and metal as if trying to jump out. I hadn't planned on jacking off before our chat tonight, but I'd need to. The woman didn't even have to look up to get me hard, didn't even have to move. All she had to do was breathe, and I wanted her.

Though the fact that there was a man in a suit sitting across from her—fucking smiling at her—tamed that desire easily enough, turning it into more of a rage than not. The world came back into view, sounds and sights of other people around me slamming into my brain. A man…across from her. Looking way too much like a date.

Motherfucker.

"Hey, Riley." Sam smiled from behind the counter, already moving toward the pastry case before I said a word. Which was good, because I wasn't sure if I could be polite right then. "I'll get your coffee going in a second. Two or three macarons today?"

"Three, please." I stared across the restaurant at Kate. What the hell was she doing here with a guy? The few times I'd happened across her path, she'd been alone or with one of her employees. This guy wasn't from city hall; he also wasn't from the island. He was too polished, too cocky. He exuded the sort of confidence that came off as arrogance. I hated the bastard on sight. Hated him more when he set his hand over her wrist and smiled as he spoke.

"That's eight-fifty." Sam interrupted my daydream of grabbing Kate right off her chair and sweeping her into my arms to get her away from the guy. Good thing, too. I wasn't sure how I'd explain staring daggers at the asshole if Kate happened to look over at me. I really needed to calm the fuck down. I also needed to scope out the situation so I could plan. I was all about the plan when it came to Kate.

I paid for my order and headed to the far corner of the shop. A low, squishy chair sat close to some bookshelves, and I folded myself into it. Why places like this couldn't have full-size furniture, I'd never know, but my knees weren't going to be happy for long sitting up under my chin. Still, the view was perfect.

Kate leaned in, looking at something laid out on the little table between her and the cocky suit guy. A lock of her blond hair swung forward, and I stared as she tucked it behind her ear in an absentminded sort of way. I nearly moaned at the sight. The motion was so normal, something I'd seen women do a million times, and yet…it was Kate.

My Kate…sort of.

She took my damn breath away, but she was with someone who seemed just as interested in her as I was. Cocky Suit Guy leaned in to match her position, his eyes on Kate instead of the paper. A smile appearing on his face. He said something, his smile widening as Kate sat back and laughed. She *laughed*. I barely got to hear her laugh because she was always so exhausted from work on Fridays, but there she was. Yukking it up with someone else.

I had totally worked the wrong plan.

When I'd moved back to Temperance Falls, I should have sought her out. Should have told her I was Banner and that I wanted to spend time with her for real. I should have made a move. Instead, I'd wanted to get my life in order and prove I was responsible by having a good job and a place to live that wasn't over a garage at my parents' house.

She was a strong, professional woman—I couldn't go in there like some kid and expect my dirty talk and muscles were going to be enough to win her. I needed to *earn* her. Or so I'd thought.

Seeing her smiling at another man made me question everything I thought I'd been doing right.

Seeing that same man get up, shake her hand, and leave the restaurant without her by his side kicked my ass into gear. She was *my* Kate, the woman I knew inside and out. The one who leaned on me to keep her satisfied. The one who told me all her fantasies and secrets, who trusted me to be her sounding board in the quiet darkness of Friday nights. I wasn't about to sit back and let some other guy swoop in. I'd fight for her if I had to, which meant she needed to know Banner wasn't just a guy on the phone.

It was time to actually meet the woman of my dreams.

Grabbing a pen left behind on a side table, I scribbled numbers on a napkin, and then headed for the front of the shop, my bag of fancy cookies in one hand and my coffee in the other. Psyching myself up so I didn't fumble all over the place when she finally saw me. It was going to be rough, for sure. I tended to lose track of my thoughts just watching her on the shitty public access channel.

Don't use the Banner voice, I reminded myself at the last minute. "Mayor Briscoe?"

Kate looked up at me and smiled that fake

politician smile I'd seen on television a hundred times. "Yes?"

Fuck me, I was screwed. Every ounce of blood in my body had redirected to my cock. There was no way she wouldn't notice *that* if she glanced down. And there was no way I could think clearly when I was practically ready to hump her leg. "I'm Riley Nash—"

"Oh, you're the latest addition to the firehouse on this side of the island, right? It's nice to meet you." She held out her hand, and I cursed myself for my cookie obsession. I made a quick switch of the bag to my coffee hand and reached out, my skin touching hers for the first time. Her palm felt soft, her grip strong. And I was fucked. Electricity shot up my arm, making me want to groan. Making me want to pull her into my arms and bury my face in her neck. To ruck up that skirt she wore and find out what secrets she hid underneath. The scent of her, the feel, the warmth—all fucking perfect for me. Just like I'd always known it would be. It was time to convince her I was just as perfect for her.

"I wanted to say I've been watching the council meetings on TV, and I think you're right about the old Temperance Falls mall. If we can utilize the current building instead of tearing it down and starting over, we should. It'd be an instant boon to the economy of the island."

Kate's smile turned more real, and her blue eyes held mine in a way that told me I'd gone the right way with this conversation. "I'm glad to hear that, Mr. Nash."

"Please, call me Riley."

"Okay, Riley. Well, thank you for stopping by to voice your approval. It means a lot. That's why I'm here, actually. I was meeting the developer to go over plans for the building." She tapped her nails against what I could see were folded floor plans, a stamp reading Huntley Group in the corner. "If this plan makes it through council review, it means a lot of jobs and housing for the island."

The developer... That meant Cocky Suit Guy wasn't a date; he was a business associate. That took a giant weight off my mind. He still looked to be flirting with my girl, though. Something I'd have to watch out for. He and Kate would be working closely together to get this deal through rezoning. Kate, another man, and closely were not words I wanted to have to deal with all at once.

"It'll make it through," I said, keeping my voice light. Keeping Banner out of the conversation so she didn't recognize me. "I have confidence in you."

Kate laughed a little, grabbing her papers and bag and readying herself to leave. "Well, I appreciate the support. I'd better get back to the office." She stood and turned my way, giving me her full attention. Stealing my breath and my voice with her beauty. "It was nice to meet you, Riley Nash."

Time to make my move.

"It was nice to meet you as well..." I paused, leaning just a little closer. Letting my voice deepen as I whispered, "Mayor Briscoe."

Kate blinked and stared, her smile falling. The

skin peeking out from the neckline of her blouse flushed a bit, and her lips fell open just enough for me to notice. Yeah, she knew that voice. "Excuse me?"

"Let me walk you out." I held out a hand toward the exit, following when she slowly started that way. She was off-balance, maybe unsure if she'd heard what she thought she had. That was good. I could do better, though.

As I opened the door for her, as she brushed past me to head outside, I leaned in a little closer. Let my voice drop a little lower. Pulled out the character of Banner just for her.

"It was good to finally meet you, Kitten."

She stood stock-still, staring at me. Her wide blue eyes practically sparking with what I hoped was excitement or desire. Only time would tell, though. Time I needed to give to her.

"I'm not a threat, and I'm not going to follow you." I dragged a finger along the back of her hand. Just for a moment before I tucked the napkin I'd written my phone number on into her palm. "I hope I'll still get to talk to you later. Directly."

With that, I turned and walked toward the firehouse. I had to. If I stayed, if I tried to explain anything, she'd bolt. My Kate was solid and sure, a risk-taker in business but completely locked off and protective of her personal life. How she'd ended up calling a phone sex line in the first place, I might never know, but I was so thankful she had.

A year of getting to know her had taught me a lot, including that she needed time to work through what

I'd just revealed. She needed to find a path to me on her own terms. I couldn't push or she'd shut down, and that wasn't an option I was willing to explore. My Plan A had blown up today, but I'd make sure Plan B came to fruition.

So I walked away.

And I prayed she'd call that night.

It was Friday, after all. Kate day. And small talk in a coffeehouse wasn't going to be enough to satisfy my need for her.

I could only hope she felt the same way.

chapter four

KATE

I STOOD FROZEN for long moments, watching Riley walk away, the unmistakable voice of Banner still ringing in my ears. Despite improbable odds, somehow the man I called to help me escape daily life on this little island lived here. And knew who I was.

Holy shit, *he knew who I was.*

That thought got my feet moving, my eyes darting to my surroundings as I took in the people milling about on Main Street. How many of them had seen the exchange? Had they thought anything of it? It wasn't unusual for me to talk with the residents as I was out and about, but my nipples didn't usually tighten from those interactions. My chest didn't flush simply from someone's nearness. No, not *someone*—just him. Banner. *Riley.*

Surely my reactions had been visible to others.

I couldn't have been the only one who'd noticed the hitch of my breath or the goose bumps on my arms. How Riley had leaned closer than was publicly appropriate…the dirty tone of his voice while he'd whispered in my ear.

A shudder ran down my spine as I crossed the street and headed into city hall. I held my head up and kept a steady pace to my office, desperate not to show a crack in my facade.

My new assistant, Lola, sat behind her desk in the outer office, fingers tapping on her keyboard. She looked up once she noticed I was there, smiling as she reached for a stack of notes on her desk. "How did the meeting go?"

I froze, my hand outstretched to grab the slips of paper. Jesus, had someone seen Riley and me together and it had already gotten back here?

Her forehead wrinkled as her brows drew down. "With Mr. Huntley? Were his plans not what you had in mind for the space?"

I tried not to let my relief show, but I couldn't help the deep exhale that escaped me. "Of course. It went well, thanks for asking." I plucked the notes from her, then nearly bolted for my door. "Please hold my calls. I have some research to do that'll take up most of the afternoon."

"Oh, I'd be happy to do that for you, if you'd like."

Lola had been working for me only a week, but I got the feeling she was a keeper of secrets. Even still, I couldn't chance handing this over to her. I could just imagine her face as I asked her to find out all the information she could on a man based only on his name and phone number. All because I was afraid said man could ruin my career with the tiny detail that I'd been paying for phone sex with him for the better part of a year.

"Thank you, Lola, but I'd like to do this particular research myself. Would you mind contacting Mr. Huntley's local assistant, Emery, and setting up another meeting for next week?"

"No problem. I'll do that now."

With a nod, I hurried into my office and shut the door before leaning against it. Allowing myself to think over the brief meeting with Banner—*Riley*. His name was Riley. When he'd first approached me, I'd appraised him the way any woman did a strange man greeting her uninvited—vaguely and with wariness.

By the time he'd let his voice drop, I'd been so shocked, I couldn't register any details. All I remembered was he was handsome. And big. Huge, actually. At least I knew he hadn't been lying about that detail—the meaning behind choosing Banner for his stage name certainly fit. I'd felt dwarfed next to him, and that wasn't easy, especially when I was wearing heels.

I pushed away from the door and took a seat behind my desk, immediately opening my laptop. Smoothing out the napkin he'd passed me, I stared at the numbers scrawled in messy black ink. No name. No information. Just ten digits. I didn't recognize the area code, so I plugged it into the search engine.

Minnesota. Minneapolis, specifically. If he lived

in Temperance Falls now—and I knew he did, as he was the newest firefighter to join the ranks at the firehouse—what was he doing with an out of state area code?

Just his name in the search engine pulled up thousands of results, but adding Temperance Falls to the search provided more of what I was looking for. It didn't take much digging to find out he'd lived here until he'd graduated from high school. He'd gone to college in Michigan, then ended up in Minneapolis at some point, though the details of that were sparse. The year of his graduation caught my eye— the same year I'd won my first public election as a councilwoman. Jesus, he was only twenty-six. Sixteen years my junior.

I sank back in my chair, eyes fluttering closed and hand settling against my throat as the hundreds of dirty secrets he'd whispered in my ear flitted through my mind. The things he'd said…the things we'd done… As if it weren't bad enough that I'd paid for phone sex, I'd done so with a man so young I felt like a dirty old woman for even recalling what had happened between us.

Pushing that feeling away, I did a quick search through the city database, finding that he'd applied for a position at the firehouse in November. Had that job brought him back to Temperance Falls after so long away?

A soft knock sounded at my door, causing me to jolt in my seat. Minimizing the screen on my laptop, I called out, "Yes?"

Lola opened the door, poking her head around to peer into my office. "Sorry to bother you, Ms. Mayor, but I wanted to check that you didn't need anything more before I left for the day."

A quick glance at my watch showed it was quarter after five. I'd been so wrapped up in researching Riley, I hadn't realized hours had passed since I'd shut myself in my office.

"No, but thank you for checking. Have a good evening, Lola."

"You, too. See you Monday." She shut the door behind her, once again giving me privacy.

Except privacy wasn't what I needed. I'd found just enough information to drive myself crazy—I knew a little more about Riley, but I didn't really *know* anything. I grabbed my phone, tapping out a quick text to Lara. If I was lucky, I could catch her before she left city hall for the day.

As I waited for her response, I cleared my browsing history and carefully tucked the napkin Riley had given me into an inside pocket of my purse. I packed up my laptop and grabbed my bag, ready to head out earlier than I had in...I couldn't even remember.

Riley had definitely thrown me for a loop, and I needed to get a handle on it. Until I did, my work would suffer, and I couldn't allow that to happen. Not now when my future as mayor hinged on this mall deal going through. I'd worked too hard to get where I was to let it slip away.

A quick knock sounded then Lara peeked in.

"Hey, you. Got your message. And I hope 'chat' was code for margaritas. El Placer?"

I laughed and slipped around my desk to give her a quick hug. "Margaritas, yes, but how about at my place instead? There's something I want to discuss away from prying ears."

"Oh, *really*." Lara lifted her brows and grinned, hooking her arm through mine as she led us out of my office. Most city hall employees clocked out at five on the dot, so the building was nearly empty as we made our way outside, our pace slow in deference to Lara's leg. It'd been months since the accident that had sent her car careening off the bridge and into the lake, but her gait was still a bit stilted. "I can't wait to hear this."

"Why don't you grab takeout from El Placer, and I'll swing by Maxine's and get everything for margaritas. Meet you at my place in twenty?"

"Pick up a couple cupcakes from Bundt and Grind, and you've got a deal."

Just the mention of the coffeehouse set off a flurry of butterflies in my stomach, Riley's voice a remembered caress against my ear, the bulk of him pressed so close I could feel his heat...

"Whoa...what's with the face?" Lara pulled me to a stop in front of her car, her forehead wrinkled in confusion. "I'm not sure if you look like you've just seen a ghost or a monster cock."

I laughed, shaking my head as I cleared the memories away. "Can we switch tasks?"

Lara raised a brow but didn't pry. "I expect this

will be part of the chat." She unlocked her door and slid into her seat. With a grin, she said, "Can't wait."

———

Lara sat on my couch, her legs outstretched, feet resting on the coffee table. Margarita in hand, she stared at me with her mouth agape. "Holy shit, Kate. I mean, *holy shit.*"

I blew out a breath, tucking a strand of hair behind my ear. "I know. It's bad, isn't it?"

"Bad?" She shook her head. "Not unless he happens to be a horrible lay. And I can't imagine he is with the mouth you've mentioned he has. If a man can get you off like that over the phone, think of what he could do when he can use more than just his voice."

"How did you jump straight to us sleeping together?" I drained my drink and set the empty glass on the coffee table. Thankfully, Lara made strong margaritas. God knew I needed every bit of tequila I could get. "Didn't you hear the part about how he knows who I am? He could ruin my career."

She waved a dismissive hand, rolling her eyes. "You're worried about nothing. He said he wouldn't share your secrets, right? Plus, he's been here for months. He's had to have known for a while, and he hasn't said a word. You know that shit would be around the island in no time." With a shrug, she took a sip of her margarita. "I think you can trust him. His mom works in the office next to mine and has given me enough Riley stories that I could fill your time for days. I can't believe the sweet boy she talks about is the same guy who's made you come like a crazy woman."

"Hey, don't make it out like I'm corrupting him. He already worked there when I started calling."

"That's not what I'm saying at all. The point I was trying to make was that he's a good guy—no one's mother would talk them up like that if they weren't."

I blanched, a thought suddenly occurring to me. "Shit, I'm old enough to be his *mom*."

"Oh my God, you are not."

"He's sixteen years younger than me!" I pointed a finger at her. "You were sixteen when you had Gen."

"Stop throwing facts at me." She finished off her margarita and placed the glass next to mine then refilled them both from the pitcher we'd had enough foresight to bring over. "Besides, it's different when you get older. Sixteen years is nothing when you're in your forties."

"But it *is* something when you're in your twenties."

"Why don't you let him decide that? I think if he thought it was a big deal, he wouldn't have said anything in the first place and just continued on as you'd been doing. If you ask me, he's interested in starting up something real. Why else would he have approached you?"

The practical part of me couldn't help but worry the other shoe had yet to drop. Couldn't help but worry what this might mean for my life, for everything I'd worked for. But my instincts—the same ones that hadn't yet failed me—said Lara was right.

"Drink this." She pushed another margarita into my hand.

"Trying to get me tipsy?" Truth was, I was already more than halfway there.

"Yep. Because it's a quarter to nine, which means it's almost time. I know you well, and I know you're going to need a little liquid courage to make that call tonight. I also know you're starting to feel the effects."

"I hope you also know I'm not calling while you're here."

She laughed, tossing her head back. "Honey, you might be my best friend, but there are some lines we just don't cross. Listening to you have phone sex is one of them."

"I'm not—"

"Maybe not. But I'd rather not stick around to find out. And anyway, I already requested a Lyft."

I took another drink, then stared at the glass, my stomach a swarm of bees. "I'm nervous, Lar."

She reached out and patted my knee. "I know you are. But I haven't steered you wrong yet, have I?"

"Um. Yeah. There was the time when—"

"*All right.* You can't say I've steered you wrong when it comes to love."

"You've never steered me one way or another."

"Exactly, so you should be listening to me the one time I am." Her phone buzzed with an incoming text, and she glanced down. "My ride's here."

She stood stiffly and pulled on her coat, her leg no doubt tight from sitting so long.

"How's your physical therapy going, by the way? We didn't even get to talk about that—or your therapist." I waggled my eyebrows at her.

With a dismissive flick of her hand, she said, "It's slow going, same old. Besides, we had more important things to talk about tonight. Next week, we can get back to me and the delicious piece of man meat helping me heal."

"That sounds good." I gave her a hug, then held the door open for her as she stepped onto the front porch.

Before she could descend the steps, she turned around. "Hey, Kate?"

"Yeah?"

"I know you're scared, but try not to be. What've you got to lose?" One last smile, and she slipped into the car idling at the curb.

I shut the door and rested my forehead against it. What did I have to lose? My career. My reputation. My life. Everything I'd ever worked for.

On the other side of that, what did I have to gain? The kind of intimacy I'd never known before Riley.

I grabbed my phone and margarita on the way upstairs, then changed into my pajamas and settled into bed. And then I stared. The numbers on my alarm clock ticked past, now coming up on 9:15. I'd never once been late for a call. Was he worried? Did he even care?

The phone sat in my lap, the same one I'd used to call him dozens of times before. Except this time, I didn't need to go through the main switchboard. This time, I had a direct line to Riley himself.

I downed half my margarita, then set the empty glass on the nightstand. With shaky hands, I grabbed the napkin Riley had given me earlier, dialed his number, and let my finger hover over the send button. Wondering if I was making the biggest mistake of my life, or if I was about to embark on something amazing.

With a deep breath, I closed my eyes and pressed send.

chapter five

NINE O'CLOCK CAME and went without my phone ringing. No standard Friday night call, no text message. Nothing. Kate had gone radio silent. I'd fucked up something fierce, and the absolute burning inside as I thought of everything I might have lost was my punishment.

I gave her fifteen minutes, the longest quarter hour of my life, before I pulled myself off the bed and started pacing. This couldn't be over. I just needed to find time to talk to her privately. I needed to explain… everything. Maybe if she gave me the opportunity to tell her how I wasn't some creepy stalker, she'd give me a chance. Or maybe it wouldn't do a damn thing because she only wanted Banner, not Riley. A thought which had me growling and tugging on my hair. I had probably fucked up this whole thing, and if she refused to talk to me, I couldn't do anything to redeem myself in her eyes.

Frustrated, I grabbed a beer from the fridge and cracked it open. I didn't normally drink alone, but it wasn't a normal night. Kate had just crushed my heart with her silence, and I deserved something to ease the pain. Before I could actually drink it, though, before I could even lift the can to my lips, my phone rang.

My motherfucking phone *actually* rang.

I raced across the room, sliding along my mattress when I dove for the phone. I didn't recognize the number on the screen, but it was local. It had to be Kate.

"Hello?" Seconds ticked by endlessly, only silence on the other end. Why did they seem to last so long? What if it wasn't her? What if—

"Hey…Riley."

My entire body went loose with relief, every inch of me sagging into the mattress. "Kate. I'm really glad you called."

"Yeah, well…I'm still not so sure."

I took a deep breath, sighing to release it. "I figured."

She stayed silent for a long time, nothing but the sound of her breathing coming through the line. But at least we were connected. There was a distance between us that hadn't been there before—which was ironic considering we were physically closer than we'd been for most of the past year—but we could bridge that. We just had to get back on firmer ground. Get back to the familiar.

"How was your day, Kitten?" I asked, resorting to her nickname, letting my voice drop into my Banner range. That deeper, rougher tone I'd always used with her. She'd liked it in the past; I could only hope it sparked something in her. Familiarity or comfort.

Kate gasped softly, then cleared her throat. "It was…fine. Good. I got a lot of things—"

"Kate." I had to stop her. That wasn't the voice I wanted. That voice was fake Kate—Mayor Kate Briscoe. I didn't want fake Kate.

"What?"

"That's not how you would have talked to me last week. I'm still me—nothing's changed except you have a face to go with the name. Now, *talk* to me. How was your day?"

It took her a few seconds to seem to get her bearings, but when she sighed, I knew I had her. "It was exhausting, and I walked way too much for the heels I'd chosen."

"Were they your pink ones?" They were, I already knew because I'd seen her, but this was our game. Our script. Common ground.

She chuckled the way she always did when I called her out. "Yes, the pink ones."

"You hate the pink ones."

"I love the pink ones."

"Fine. Your feet hate the pink ones." I couldn't hold back my smile. This…this was us. This was what we did. This was how I'd fallen in love with her. I just needed to make her see that she loved me too, even if she didn't know it yet.

"They do. They really do." She sighed, and I reached down to rest my hand on my cock. More out of habit than anything. Her voice created a Pavlovian response in me. One word made me hard. A few sentences had me leaking for her. I bet she had the same response. I bet every sentence in Banner's voice caused her pussy to grow wetter. More swollen. More…needful.

Fuck, I wanted her beside me for this. "Tell me more. Tell me everything. I want to know about your day so I can make you forget it."

Kate took her time finding her words, taking a deep breath before finally speaking. "This…guy… came up to me in the coffeehouse."

Oh. Okay…diving right in. "Yeah? Was he hot?"

Her laugh was such a fucking gift. "Yes, but that's not important."

"Of course it is, but I'll cede to your point. You were saying?"

"You're kind of naughty tonight."

I squeezed my cock harder and gave it a good tug, loving the way she said naughty. She was right, I was. But only for her. "Yup. Now tell me, why is that moment important? What did you think when he approached you?"

"At first, I thought he was a constituent wanting to talk about an issue."

"Sounds reasonable. But he wasn't, was he? Not really."

"No, he wasn't. He's…" She went silent, and I held my breath. Waiting to see how she saw me, knowing these next words were so very vital to our future. "He's someone I care for, someone I trust. But he really took me by surprise."

Hearing her admission—knowing she cared for me—about set my damned soul on fire. "In a good way or a bad way?"

"Bad…at first. His presence shook me." Her voice sounded small, completely unlike her. She wasn't exaggerating—I'd probably shaken her right down to her pink shoes.

"I'm sure he didn't mean to do that," I said, hoping my sincerity came through. Fighting back the feelings of regret at having handled our first meeting so poorly.

"Riley—"

"Banner." I wasn't sure what made me interrupt her, but it felt right. It felt like the right path to stay where we'd been for so long. "For just a little longer, let's be Banner and Kitten, okay?"

She sighed again but eventually gave me a quiet, "Okay."

I'd take it. Hell, at that point, I'd take anything. Even if that meant staying as Banner and Kitten. I'd hate it, but it was better than no contact.

Knowing I needed to pull off quite a show, I dug deep for all my Kate knowledge. Dropped my voice into the lowest range I could and ran my hand over my cock a few times to remind me what we were doing here. "Just hearing the phone ring got me hard for you, Kitten. Did you know that? The ringtone of my damn phone makes me as horny as a teenager."

"I didn't," she said, her voice breathy and uneven. Yeah, she was with me. Time to turn up the heat.

"Are you undressed yet? Or are you still wearing your suit?"

"No, I changed before I called. I'm in one of my camis."

I groaned, flicking the head of my cock on a pass. "Fuck, I love that. It's pink, isn't it? You like your little bits of pink under all that stiff business wear."

She chuckled, the rustle of fabric in the background a sure sign she was getting comfortable. Maybe on her bed or couch. Maybe getting naked for me. God, I hoped she got naked for me.

"I do like my pink," she said, something about the way she said that last word calling up a memory. A musician she liked had an album about pink, some sort of play on words to mean pussy instead of color. Yeah, I liked that idea. I liked that a lot.

"I'd like to see your pink, baby," I said, growling through the words, nearly fist-pumping when I heard her little gasp of pleasure. She knew where I'd gone with that reference, knew the connotations. "We'll get there someday. We'll get to a place where you'll trust me enough to spread those long legs of yours and give me what I've been craving. For now, why don't you relax and let me talk to you? Just talk like always. Let me get you off with my words."

She groaned, a definite sign of her increasing arousal. "I have so many questions, though."

"I know. We can do both, right? Get to know the pieces we didn't before, while doing what we always do? I think it'd be easier that way. A slower transition from Banner and Kitten to…others. Don't you think we can do both?"

"Okay…yeah. Yeah. We can do that."

"Good. Then ask me a question. I'll answer it as Riley, then go back to Banner for a few to remind you I'm still the same guy who wants nothing more than to bury my face in your pussy and make you scream my name."

She released a nervous chuckle, her only response for a long minute. I began to wonder if I should give her another push when she finally asked, "Do you meet all your clients?"

"Fuck no. I've never done this before." Time for a little truth, a small admission on my part. "Besides, there are no others to meet. You're my only client."

"What?"

"It's only been you calling me. I stopped taking on anyone else shortly after our first conversation. No one made me feel the way you do, and it seemed wrong to talk to others. You're the one I wanted, the only one I moved my entire life for."

Her silence wasn't as weighted as before, but it was longer than I'd hoped for. "How long have you known?"

"Six months, maybe. I didn't search you out, if that's your concern." I jacked my cock a few times, nice and slow, letting my fingers circle the head on every upward pass. "You were on a newscast airing in Minneapolis, something about the scandal at the college. I heard your voice on the television, and I knew. I'd know your voice anywhere. Just like you'd know mine." I gave her a moment to take that in, to absorb the truth of my words, before twisting the conversation just a little. "You like my voice, don't you? I bet I made you wet today when I whispered in your ear, even if you weren't ready for me. You're ready now though, aren't you? How about you lie back and spread your legs for me, baby? We're going to get serious here in a few."

"Banner." She groaned softly, the sound making my hips jerk in response. "Minneapolis…where you lived after college, right?"

I froze, my brain stuttering. Had I told her… No, I hadn't.

"How'd you know that?" I nearly laughed as Kate sat silent, neither of us even breathing. "Have you been Googling me, Mayor Briscoe?"

"That probably wasn't very professional of me, was it?"

"Fuck professional. I prefer the unprofessional side of you. Everyone gets to see the mayor—I get to see the real you." Or talk to, but I didn't want to call that out. Didn't want to ruin the moment. "Why don't you slide your hand over your breast for me, baby? Give your nipple a little tug. That's what I'd do if I were there, though it'd be with my teeth. I bet your nipples are sweet as candy, aren't they? I bet they're sensitive, too. You think I could make you come with just my hands and mouth on your breasts? Think I could suck your tits until you trembled all over? I'd like to try."

"Oh God." Her voice came out as a sigh, as a needy little plea. One I wanted to answer.

"That's it, Kitten. Now work your hand lower. I want to hear you moaning for me. I want to know your fingers are playing with your pussy when I answer the next question. Are you ready yet? Are you wet for me already?"

"I'm…getting wet," she said, her voice stuttering. She'd normally be soaked by now, telling me all about how much she wanted to feel me. But *getting* wet was better than not at all. It was progress. I'd take it.

"Hmmm, getting wet. I can work with that. You keep rubbing that pussy. Give that clit a few soft pinches and pretend it's my lips and tongue on you. I'd baby that pussy if I were there, waking her up slowly. Teasing you until you grabbed my hair and begged me to suck on your clit. You would, too. You're a greedy girl. Now ask another question as I dream what that sweet pussy tastes like."

"Shit." She practically hissed the word. I stroked my cock from base to tip. Wishing I were there to see her. Wishing it really was me touching her. Kissing her. Loving her. Making her come. "Why did you come back?"

My girl went right for the meat of the issue, didn't she? I shouldn't have been surprised. Kate was always good in business mode—direct and succinct. Guess it was my moment of truth.

"You," I said, closing my eyes and praying she didn't hang up. "I never felt a connection to anyone the way I did to you on that first call. It was…

explosive. When I figured out who you were and how your life intersected with mine, I knew it was a sign for me to come home. It was time to quit fucking around and start living my life. One I wanted to share with you." I stretched out, focusing on the ceiling. Teasing myself as I fell back into my role as Banner. "Slip a finger inside yourself. Gotta get that pussy nice and stretched for me. I wouldn't want to hurt you with my cock, now would I? I want everything to feel good for you. Always."

She laughed lightly, still a little breathy. Sounding slightly distracted. "This is crazy. You know that, right?"

"I do, but so is us talking on the phone when we could be doing this in person. I could have my tongue deep inside you right now. Do you realize that? I could have you open before me. I'd eat you like a woman should be eaten, too. I'd make you come so hard before I even thought of getting mine. Are your fingers still in your pussy, baby? Are you pretending they're me?"

"Yes," she whispered. "But I don't think I can… finish. I don't think we can keep doing this."

"Don't." I clung to the phone, not sure how far that *we* went. Not willing to give her the chance to think I'd just give her up. "Don't say we can't, or throw obstacles up that aren't really there. I know you, Kate. I *know* you, and you know me. We've spent a year getting to know everything about each other—that has to count for something."

"Sometimes it's not that easy," she said, sounding

truly regretful and almost sad. "If you know me as well as you say you do, then you know my career means the world to me. And this…whatever we have… It could blow up in my face. It could cost me everything I've worked for."

"I disagree. I'm a firefighter, for fuck's sake. People love first responders. It's practically un-American not to date me."

She huffed a laugh. "What you are, Riley, is twenty-six."

"Which means jack shit." I sat up, unable to keep going with the whole Banner thing. "I'm not a kid, Kate. I'm an adult making sound decisions. My family is known here; I'm known here. No one's going to talk shit about us because there's nothing to say—we're two adults who found a connection and are exploring it. End of. Besides, I won't let anyone stand in your way. Your career would be safe with me by your side. I'd make damn sure of it."

"Banner—"

"Riley. If we're talking real life, I'm Riley, and you're Kate, though you'll always be my Kitten."

Kate sighed. "Riley, I just don't know."

"You do, or else you wouldn't have called. You do know or else you wouldn't have followed my instructions to play with your pussy. You're good and wet now, aren't you? You're turned on and slick for me, right?"

A long pause, longer than the ones before. Long enough I worried she'd say no. But she didn't. "Yes. But I don't—"

"That's us, Kate. That's our connection. Right now, it seems solely physical, but it's not. My words get you off because I care about you, because I know you. Because I understand what you need better than you do yourself sometimes, so I can give you what you truly want. We can move that into real life. I can spoil you as rotten as you deserve to be, and we can be together without giving people a reason to judge us. We can at least try."

Kate sighed again, still pausing. Leaving me on the edge of my seat for far too long. "What if we fail?" she finally asked.

"We won't," I replied, refusing to let her have even a sliver of doubt. "I won't let us."

"If people find out—"

"I'll put the smackdown on anyone who dares to say a word against us, as will the rest of my family. As will every guy at the firehouse. We protect our own, Kate. You'd have a team of people having your back."

"Riley, I'm just not—"

"Meet me tonight." Desperate, I threw out the only thing I had left. The only bullet in my chamber. She didn't say anything, so I plowed on. Hoping like hell I didn't scare her off. "I know it's crazy, but we've finally seen each other in person, we know who the other is. Meet me tonight. You're wound up, I'm wound up…let's see if we can go from fake fucking over the phone to something real. See if we can transition to something tangible. Let me prove we can."

"You can't come here. If someone sees—"

"I know a place. It's private. No one will see us. I just want to be with you for a little while. I want to talk to you in person. To see your face."

Another fucking pause. My God, the woman was going to give me a heart attack. "You promise it's secluded?"

"Swear to God, no one will be there. No one will see us together."

"Okay, I'm going to take a leap and trust you," she said, making me jump up from the bed and finally throw that fist pump. "Where do you want me?"

"Riding my face, but we'll get to that." I chuckled when she huffed a laugh. "Meet me at the old lighthouse."

"What for? It's a construction site."

"I know. I've been working there on my off days at the firehouse to keep busy. Meet me there. I promise, it'll be worth it."

She hummed as if thinking it over. "I can't promise I'll stay for long."

"Give me five minutes. That's all I ask."

"Fine. I can be there in half an hour."

Motherfucking win. "I'll be waiting."

I made it to the spot in twenty minutes, not wanting Kate to end up alone in the dark. She was a little late, turning into the lot about thirty-five minutes after we'd hung up. I assumed because of her nerves. Kate was punctual as fuck in real life—she had to be on edge.

She parked beside me, turning off the engine and sitting in the dark for a few seconds before opening her door. Brave fucking woman, she crawled out and stood tall as she faced me. As she looked me right in the eyes.

For the first time in my memory, I no longer felt lost. Something crackled between us. Something sparked and came to life. There was an energy, a pull. A tension that made me want to surrender to it. She was my home, my true north, my guiding light…all those corny as fuck analogies about the woman you were meant to spend your life with. She was all of them.

We stood in the dark, the only light from the interior of her car. Kate's eyes held mine for the longest time before swooping lower, taking me in. Almost… inspecting me. I couldn't blame her—I'd known she was Kate. This was her first time really getting the chance to see the man she knew as Banner. So I stood still, and if someone had pressed me on it, I'd have to lie to say I wasn't flexed just a bit. I couldn't help it. Her eyes owned me, and I made sure I looked as good as I could. I needed to make an impression, this time a good one. I wanted her to like what she saw because I sure as hell did.

Tall and curvy, she struck a strong pose. Something in the way she planted her feet—no longer in the pink heels—or the way her shoulders stayed straight and back. Something in her screamed confidence. It turned me on, for sure. I couldn't have looked away if I'd tried, and I didn't want to. This was it; I could feel it. This was the night we moved forward.

This was the first step toward our future together.

We stared for what felt like hours, not moving.

Barely breathing. Until finally, finally, she sighed in a way I knew meant she was feeling what I was. That she recognized our connection. That we were beginning something amazing.

"Riley," she whispered, the tone of her voice like a starter's pistol.

I broke. I grabbed her, pulling her to me and planting my lips on hers. Fusing us together the only way I could. That first kiss was too strong, too rough, but I couldn't control myself. This woman was my dream, my wish, my future…and I'd do everything in my power to keep her with me.

Her tongue swept into my mouth, and I groaned. She tasted like citrus and Kate, something completely her that I couldn't have described to save my life. Her arms around my neck anchored me, her body pressing up against mine the force I needed to hold her to me. The wind blew strong and cold, but it didn't matter. Nothing mattered. All I cared about was the feel of her lips under mine, the warmth of her body as she pressed herself against me. The world could fuck right off for all I cared.

"Are you ready?" I asked when I finally pulled away. When I finally found the will to release her lips from mine. Her eyes gazed up at me, all wide and shocked. Beautiful. "Are you ready to move on from Banner and come to Riley? Will you let me show you how we're one and the same?"

A pause, that brain of hers probably turning over every possibility. Every chance of a misstep. Finally, she nodded, and I was done.

"Then come with me, Kitten. I want to get to know you, and we're sure as hell not doing that outside."

chapter six

KATE

RILEY PULLED ME along behind him, my lips still tingling from his kiss. I hadn't been expecting that, hadn't expected the immediate connection I'd felt as soon as his skin had touched mine. Then again, I hadn't been expecting Riley.

His hand radiated heat against mine as we climbed the back steps of the lighthouse—the lighthouse he'd slipped us into using a *borrowed* code for the electronic lock on the back door. The lighthouse that had a bright red NO TRESPASSING sign on the door. I couldn't believe I was doing this. This kind of thing didn't even register on my radar—had *never*. Even as a teenager, I'd been a rule follower, methodical in everything I did. No drugs, no underage drinking, no missed curfew—hell, I'd never even skipped class. If it wasn't part of the plan, I didn't do it.

But I wasn't a teenager anymore—I was the damn mayor. Everything about this situation was ridiculous, and yet there I was. Sneaking into the lighthouse with a man sixteen years my junior to do... God, I didn't even know what Riley had planned. Which somehow only made this more illicit. What exactly did I think was going to happen here? What was I going to *allow* to happen?

Honestly? After the phone call? After that kiss in the parking lot? Anything he wanted. *Everything*.

"You still with me, Kate?" He looked back at me, the breadth of his shoulders blocking out the light from above. No denying the fact that his body had mine humming with awareness. With pleasure.

I squeezed his fingers, giving him a smile. "I'm with you."

And I was... Being with him, even just over the phone, had been the only time I'd ever been able to shut off my brain. I'd relished that time, relished the freedom I'd felt at giving up control, even for a little while. I'd accepted his offer to meet because of the possibility that what we had together could extend beyond two voices connecting over the phone. I hadn't been able to stop thinking about what could be awaiting me if he actually *touched* my body.

The things he'd said over the phone tonight had been everything I'd been too scared to consider. And he'd been right—we had a crazy connection that would no doubt only grow more explosive in person.

"Almost there. I wasn't thinking about the fact

that you wore the pink heels today when I suggested we climb up here. How're your toes?"

As if I were thinking about my feet at a time like this. Still, I couldn't help swooning a little at the fact that he apparently was. He always seemed to be thinking about my comfort…my pleasure. "No worse than they were at five o'clock. I'll be fine."

"Good. That's good. Let me take care of that needy little pussy, then I can kiss all over your feet and make them feel better."

Jesus. The things he said…the spark in his eyes as he said them? I wasn't sure how much longer I'd be able to stand if he kept talking to me like that.

Thankfully, we didn't have much farther to go. Nearly at the top of the lighthouse, we approached a curved landing with a single door along one side. Riley punched another—no doubt borrowed—code into the electronic lock for the room. Once the light went green and the door popped open, he squeezed my fingers, looked back at me with a smile lighting up his face, and tugged me along behind him.

My low heels clicked on the wide wooden planks of the floor as I crept inside the room, staring at the stunning space. The ceilings towered above us, making the small room feel open and airy, and the exposed brick along one of the walls exuded warmth, even with no furniture or decorations inside. A fireplace sat along the far wall, between the floor-to-ceiling windows.

I approached one of them and stared into the darkness. During the day, these would no doubt give a breathtaking view of the lake. Now, though, it was nearly pitch black, except for a few lights flashing in the distance.

"I can't believe I didn't know this was up here."

"Jackson uncovered this room when he bought the lighthouse." Riley slipped right behind me, his body brushing against mine. I wanted to lean into him, wanted to turn around and kiss him— he hadn't been the only one fantasizing about it for a year. But then he settled his hands on my shoulders, kneading the tension away. "This room had been storage originally, but it's too nice for that. The windows were already here, perfectly placed. Once Jackson saw the view from them, he decided to turn this into a single room B&B."

"It's beautiful."

"You're beautiful."

I looked back at him, a small smile playing on my lips. "I bet you say that to all the girls."

He shook his head, his eyes full of earnest intensity. "Just you." He dropped his hands from my shoulders, tracing his fingers down my arms, his thumbs brushing the edges of my breasts on the way down. Just a whisper. A tease. Still, my nipples tightened in response. "Since the first call, it's only been you."

I didn't know what to say to that, had no idea how to respond. It'd been the same for me. Even if I'd had interest in dating, anyone else would've paled in comparison to the relationship Riley and I had forged over the phone. One undeniably filled with chemistry and passion, but also full of understanding and companionship. I could tell him anything—it was just a bonus how easily and thoroughly he could get me off.

He cupped my face in his hands. Rubbed his thumbs along my cheeks, his eyes darting all over my face. Like he was studying me. Like he was cataloging everything in his memory to refer to later.

And then… Then he lowered his head, his lips meeting mine in a soft kiss. Sweet, almost innocent. But nothing about us was sweet or innocent, and he proved that when he stroked his tongue along my bottom lip, groaning when I opened to him, and pushed me back against the wall. He pressed his body along mine as he took my mouth, his tongue sliding against mine in a more polished approach than the hungry, greedy kiss we'd shared downstairs.

I let him lead, let him take me where he wanted me to go, lost to everything but him. Riley kissed exactly like he spoke—with unbridled confidence and power. Without words, he told me he knew what I needed. And he was going to give it to me.

He caressed me over my clothes with desperate hands, his thumbs brushing my taut nipples before he gripped my hips. Tugged me closer. Maybe feeling as desperate for me as I was for him. The hard length of his cock pressed against me as he rocked forward, his harsh groan echoing in the space.

He let me break away panting as he trailed kisses down my neck, one hand cupping my breast, his thumb tracing circles around my nipple. Into my ear, he whispered, "Are you still wet, Kitten?"

His voice sent shivers down my spine, causing me to arch my back…press closer. Between his words over the phone, the anticipation of what was coming as I'd driven over here, and his hands all over me, it was safe to say my panties were a mess.

"You know I am."

His lips curved against my cheek, the bristles of his day-old beard tickling my face. "I do know, don't I? I've heard exactly how wet you get. Now I want to feel it."

I groaned, letting my head fall to the side as he kissed a path along my neck, scraped his teeth against my jaw. Cupped my breasts in his hands and squeezed.

Sliding his fingers to the V neck of my dress, he tugged it away from my body. "You gonna let me take this off you?"

I breathed out a laugh and lifted my arms in response. No longer interested in hesitancy.

"That's my girl."

In one fluid motion, he stripped me of the dress, tossing it somewhere off to the side. I stood naked before him, the tiny scraps of black lace I wore the only things keeping him from seeing all of me. I tried not to fidget as he stared, but I couldn't help it. Yes, I went to the gym. Yes, I tried to eat healthy. But at forty-two, I was a far cry from the twentysomethings Riley was no doubt used to, and no amount of planks would change that.

But as I looked at him devouring me with his eyes,

saw the fire there, every ounce of self-consciousness I had evaporated at the sight.

"Jesus, Kate," he said, his voice low and gritty as he rubbed a hand along the dark blond scruff at his jaw. He reached out, running his hands across my shoulders, down my arms, traced his fingers along the swell of my breasts. "I knew you were sexy as fuck in your suits, but this…" He shook his head. "You're so goddamn beautiful."

Dropping to his knees in front of me, he gripped my waist and slipped his hands around to cup my ass, digging his fingers into my flesh. So greedy in his caresses. Making me feel wanted…cherished. He lowered his head, his lips brushing over each hip, then he dipped down, running his nose along the front of my panties before placing a kiss directly above my clit. Sending a shudder through my entire body. "I've been starving for this. A fucking year of wondering what you'd feel like against my tongue, and now I finally get a taste."

I reached out, brushing the hair back from his face, and raised an eyebrow. "Just one?"

His grin was pure devil. "We'll start with one. But don't worry—I'll make it good for you. One for me might be six for you. I'll make sure you're sloppy wet before I slide my cock inside this pretty pussy."

Jesus. I wanted that. *Desperately*. He left me only long enough to grab a couple drop cloths from a box next to the fireplace. Then he pressed a button, and the flames inside the glass enclosure came to life.

I breathed out a laugh, warmth running through

me at how nice he was trying to make this for me. For us. "Well, you definitely have the whole seduction thing down."

Riley spread the tarps on the ground, stacking them to provide some padding. "It's not what you deserve, but I know you won't care. I know you feel like I do—like you don't want to wait another day to see what us in person is like." Sitting up on his knees, he extended his hand, beckoning me closer.

He was right. I'd never thought my time with Banner would extend beyond the phone. But now that I was there, now that the flesh and blood person behind the words Banner spoke…the emotions and thoughts and feelings he'd shared with me… Now that he was in front of me, desperate for me, I couldn't remember a time I'd been this turned on. Electricity sparked under my skin, the anticipation between us a living, breathing thing. But still, I wanted more.

Without hesitation, I approached him, stopping only when his hands on my waist halted me. He trailed openmouthed kisses down the curve of my stomach as he reached behind me and unhooked my bra. No longer worried about what he'd think when he saw me naked, instead only desperate for him to. With my bra tossed in the direction of my dress, I waited. This was Riley's show, and we both knew it. I was just along for the ride.

"I should've known you'd have perfect pink-tipped tits. Like gumdrops. C'mere and let me get a taste." He didn't tease me with soft kisses, didn't taunt me with barely there strokes of his tongue. Instead, he gripped my hips, holding me exactly where he wanted me, and latched on, hollowing his cheeks as he sucked my nipple deeply into his mouth.

I moaned and arched against him, my fingers threading through his hair, holding him to me. Begging without words for him never to leave. "Riley, *God…*"

He groaned against my breast, his eyes flaring as he stared up at me. Pulling back, he circled my nipple with his tongue before blowing against it. "Hearing my name fall from your lips is fucking heaven, did you know that? All these months, I've been dying to hear you say it. It's fucking perfect. Best part is, we both know you're gonna scream it before the night's over, don't we? My Kitten's a screamer."

He licked between the valley of my breasts as he sank down on his knees and tugged off my panties. Steadying myself on one of his massive shoulders, still covered in his heavy flannel, I lifted each leg in turn as he removed my underwear. Wanting to do nothing but tug off that bulky shirt he wore and see what was hidden underneath.

When he looked up, when he refocused on me, his entire body went stiff. I stood in front of him, completely bare, and reveled in the heat in his eyes as he took in every inch of me. "Fuck, you're gorgeous," he said, still not moving. "Do you have any idea how many times I've jerked my cock to the idea of licking your pussy? How often I've thought about you riding my face?"

I brushed a hand down his cheek, his stubble

rough against my fingertips. What would that feel like against my thighs? Against my pussy? "Tell me."

"Every goddamn day. I wake up hard as stone because I dream of it. You've been my only fantasy for months, and the reality of your body has blown my Imagination Kate out of the water." He tugged me down until I was on my knees and took my mouth in another all-consuming kiss. Sure and solid, he caressed me with his hands, stroking, guiding until I was laid out on the cloths, bared before him. And then he pressed against my inner thighs, opening me to him.

"Spread for me, Kitten. Let me get a good look at you."

"I want to look at you, too." I reached for him, intent on helping him out of his clothes. Wanting nothing more than to feel his skin against mine.

Instead of letting me reach fabric, he grabbed my hand and brought it down, pressing it against his denim-covered cock. His very hard, very thick, very holy-shit-is-that-real cock. "You feel that? That's a solid year of pent-up desire to be inside you. If I lose a single piece of clothing, I'll never be able to hold back. I'll be balls deep before I can get my first taste of you. I've talked about all I'm going to do to this pussy for a year. I want to take my time now."

Before I could argue, before I could tell him that as much as I ached to feel his tongue on my clit, I wanted him inside me more, he dropped down, his broad shoulders parting my legs, and spread me wide with his thumbs. With a groan, he dove forward and covered my pussy with his mouth.

Gasping, I arched against him and gripped his shoulders, hoping it would anchor me. Because this…this, I hadn't been expecting. Receiving oral had never been my favorite thing, but then again, I'd never before had Riley going at me like a starving man. He devoured me, licking up one side and down the other before sucking my clit between his lips.

He pulled back on a groan, replacing his tongue with his fingers, rubbing tight circles around my clit. "I knew it." He shook his head, staring at where I was spread open for him. Then he leaned down, swiping his tongue through my slit once more, like he couldn't help himself. "Knew I'd be addicted to your taste. Fuck, I'm going to want to eat you every goddamned day."

Without another word, he tossed my legs over his shoulders and engulfed me in his mouth, his tongue drawing figure eights against my pussy. His hands were everywhere, stroking up my sides, squeezing my breasts, cupping my ass, and bringing me closer to his mouth.

All words left my head, only unintelligible mumblings spilling from my lips as he devoured me like I was his last meal. He wrapped his hands around the tops of my thighs, his fingers digging in so hard I knew I'd have bruises tomorrow. But I didn't care. I didn't care, not when he was looking up at me like he was, his face buried in my pussy, his eyes locked on mine. Not when he gripped me so hard he actually lifted me off the ground, trying to bring me closer.

"Don't stop, don't stop, Riley… Oh God, I'm gonna come…"

He groaned against me, his eyes never leaving mine. I kept mine open and locked on his for as long as I could…until my orgasm swept me away. With his hair gripped in my hands, I rocked my hips against his face, gasping as I pulsed and throbbed and came all over his tongue.

Once the last aftershocks had gone through my body, he lifted his head. "One down." He grinned and wiped a thumb across his shiny, wet bottom lip. "I want to feel the next one on my fingers. Gotta get you ready to take my cock, don't we?" He slipped his fingers inside me, first two, then three, thrusting them deep, exactly how he knew I loved. "Hmmm, tight and hot. Just like I knew it'd be. You know how many times I've been jealous of some silicone and batteries, baby? Not tonight, though. Tonight it's all me. My fingers." He bent down, licking around where his fingers disappeared inside me. "My tongue. My fucking cock."

"Riley…I'm ready. I'm—" I gasped, arching my back as he hit a spot inside me. "Please, I'm ready for you."

"Not yet. I wanna look at you for a minute. Do you have any idea how beautiful you are right now? So greedy, writhing against my hand as I fuck you with my fingers. You're stunning."

God, I couldn't remember the last time I'd been

this close to coming again so soon after my last orgasm, and yet Riley had gotten me there with ease. Because of his words. Because of his skills. Because of *him*.

He gave my inner thigh a love nip as he held me open, resting his lips against me. And he smiled. "Your thighs are shaking. Are you that close already? Should I give you a little more? Push you right over that edge?" Without waiting for me to respond, he brought his other hand down and strummed his thumb over my clit. "I'm going to want to fuck you next. Are you ready for that? Ready to feel my cock inside you instead of all those toys you've told me about? No silicone or batteries here, baby. Just me. Is that what you want?"

"God *yes*," I moaned, wanting to feel him against me, *inside* me. "Riley, please. Please, please, please…"

"Mmm…love to hear you beg." He thrummed faster against my clit, curled his fingers inside, brushing against the spot that made my hips jerk.

And then I was gone, lifting my hips toward him and pulsing around his fingers, head tossed back as I moaned his name.

"Fuck, yeah, Kitten. That's it. I can feel you gripping my fingers. So fucking good."

It could've been seconds or minutes later when I blinked my eyes open, still trying to catch my breath. Riley hovered over me, his hands on either side of my shoulders. "God, you're beautiful when you come." He leaned down, sucking my bottom lip into his mouth before releasing it with a pop. "Can't wait to see that look while you're riding my cock."

chapter seven

SWEET FUCKING HELL, naked Kate was something to see. Something to behold. And the way her face twisted as she neared her orgasm, the way that moment of pleasure-pain showed so clear in those last few seconds before the tension broke and her pussy clenched…stunning. Nothing better. I wanted to live in that moment, to bury myself inside her and never come out.

But first, I needed to get undressed.

"Did I ever tell you I tried being a stripper-for-hire?" I sat back on my knees, spreading them to keep her thighs apart. To keep that wet, plump pussy in my view.

"No," Kate said with a laugh, looking relaxed and calm. Sated. Not gonna lie—that really helped my ego.

"It was when I started working the phone sex gig. I figured if I could turn someone on with my voice, I sure as hell could with my body." I tugged off my flannel and dropped it behind me before grabbing the neck of my white undershirt and yanking it over my head. "I was so fucking wrong."

"What happened?"

I rose to my feet, working on the fastenings of my jeans until they hung open. My cock bulged right out the flap, probably obscene as hell and soaked at the tip. Good. I wanted Kate to get a look at what was coming.

"Well…" I said, shoving the denim down my legs. I hadn't thrown my boxers on before I'd left, so I was already bare. Bare and ready for her. "I could strip okay. I could even give my ass a shake and get the ladies yelling."

"I believe that." Her saucy little smile about unmanned me.

I smirked and dropped back to the floor, kicking my jeans off the rest of the way. Kate stared at my lap, at my cock. Looking hungry. The fucker twitched as she watched him, probably as attuned to our girl's body as I was.

"What I couldn't do was what came next." I moved to sit with my back against the wall, tugging Kate with me, pulling her into my lap until she straddled me. Her pussy sat warm and wet against my skin, and I shivered at the sensation even as I handed her the condom I'd pulled from my pocket. She tore it open and rolled it on without a single pause. Meanwhile,

I tried to keep the thought that she was touching my cock from taking over my brain. "Jesus, your fingers feel good." Hip thrust…couldn't help it. "Anyway, I was in a room with all these women, practically naked, and I froze. Totally clueless as to what to do next."

"So let me get this straight," Kate said, placing her hands on my shoulders and rocking slightly as if searching for a more comfortable position. Which happened to be sitting squarely on my cock, not that I minded. "You were paid to perform, but you… what? Made cookies?"

"No, I ran out of the house wearing a gold thong, holding my jeans in my hands. I didn't know what to do, so I ghosted." I grabbed her hips and raised my legs to form a support behind her. Pushed her back until she was sprawled out before me. "I'm not running tonight."

"I would hope not."

"Hey, Kate?" I ran a finger down the middle of her chest, all the way to her belly button. Simple, soft. Perfect.

"Yeah?"

"I sure as fuck know what to do with *you*."

I grabbed her by the waist, lifting her just enough to line up my cock with the heart of her pussy, and then I pulled her down. Her warmth enveloped me, followed closely by an explosion of nerve endings as she engulfed me inside her body. I groaned and she gasped, both of us tightening our hold on the other. Fuck, I thought her pussy had felt good on my fingers. Tight and hot and soaked for me. This? This was so much more. And if the way the goose bumps rose on her skin as I shifted my hips a few inches was any indication, Kate agreed. Her pussy was positively made for my cock.

"God, Riley." She tried to roll forward, but I pushed her back instead. I wanted her spread before me, wanted to watch. So I settled her against my thighs and rocked my hips to thrust into her. And I died a little bit with every inch I gained, with every pulse of her walls around me, with the sight of her pink lips swallowing me up. Shit, this was going to be quick. I needed to make it good.

I also needed to distract myself. "Know what this position is called?"

"Amazing?" She trembled as I brought my hands to her breasts. As I kneaded and squeezed and tweaked each nipple in turn.

"The chair limbo. I'm the chair, and you get to limbo all over my cock." I punctuated my words with another deep thrust, earning a solid groan from my girl. "I like to watch. This view of my cock sliding inside of you? I've been imagining it for a fucking year—I deserve to look, don't you think? But I also like access to you. Your shoulders." I ran a finger up one arm, all the way to her neck. "Your tits with those cotton-candy nipples." I brought my hand to my mouth so I could lick my thumb before dropping it back down. Flicking her nipple to wet it just a little then giving it a good pinch.

Kate jerked and groaned, still riding my cock.

Still swallowing me with her pussy. "Riley, please," she moaned, but I wasn't done yet. Wasn't ready to surrender.

"My favorite, though," I said, dragging my thumb along her stomach. Lower still, past her hip bone. Over her mound. Lifting it to my lips once more to get it good and wet. And ready. "My favorite thing about this position is how spread you are. Your clit is completely on display, did you know that?"

I ran my thumb around the little pearl, hanging on to her thigh with my other hand as she jumped and yelped. "Wide open and all for me. How could I not love this position? I get to fuck you and explore you, all at once. It's perfect."

"Oh God." Kate groaned, curling her body in slightly, her thighs trembling. "I'm gonna come again. I want…I want…"

"I know what you need, baby." I pushed up, settling her deeper onto my lap, thrusting inside her at a faster pace as my thumb circled her clit. "Let go, Kate. I've got you. Come for me so I can fuck you hard. You know you want that, want to feel me pound into that sloppy, wet pussy. You're not some sweet thing, baby. You're just as dirty as me. And you like it just as rough as I do."

I pressed down on her clit, giving her the pressure I knew she needed. She came with a quick scream, her head thrown back and her thighs holding me in place. And fuck, did she come. So damn tight, so damn strong. Clenching and squeezing and pulling me inside her deeper as she writhed in my lap. Her pussy stretching all the way around my cock as she arched back.

Motherfucking beautiful.

Before she was done, before I lost control at the feel of her pussy milking me, I dragged her against my chest and rolled us. Pinning her beneath me. Jackhammering my hips like some high school punk. I couldn't help it, though. I'd made sure she got hers, had held off on my own pleasure to guarantee I'd taken care of my woman. It was my turn, and my cock wanted hard and fast. I'd made him wait a year for this. Who was I to say no?

"Riley...yes." Kate held on to my shoulders, her legs around my hips. Riding my deep thrusts like a fucking pro.

I growled and bit her shoulder, unable to resist. Needed to have a piece of her inside me. Shoving deep, arching my back and groaning toward the ceiling, I came with a jolt that sent tingles all the way to my toes. Came so hard, something bright erupted behind my closed eyes.

I came in a manner worthy of a woman like Kate, because it was her ingrained sensuality that pushed me right over the edge.

"That was..." Kate moaned as I rolled, trying to keep us connected but not wanting to crush her. She seemed so small under me.

"I'd say stupendous or best ever, but I'll go with perfect if that's the word you choose."

"A little cocky, huh?"

I couldn't help it. I thrust deep once more,

groaning as the tingles shot through my spine again. "There's nothing little about me or my cock."

That earned me a laugh, one that sent twinges down my legs since we were still connected. A status that needed to change. I never wanted to leave her pussy, but I had to.

I pulled out, clutching the base of the condom to keep it tight. Once I'd disposed of the fucker, I lay back down with her. Curled my body around hers and cradled her against my chest. "We did this backward."

"How so?"

"Well, I knew how you sounded when you orgasmed before we met, knew how dirty your mouth could be before our first kiss, and now know how close being inside your pussy is to heaven before I've taken you on a date. We should rectify that."

"I don't think you can rewind sex."

I chuckled, rolling her under me a little. "No, but I wouldn't mind. That chair limbo was hot."

"Yeah, it was."

I kissed her nose. "I'll remember that. What I meant, though, was that I should at least take you to dinner. And soon. What do you think about tomorrow night? I've heard Nonno Pino's has amazing Italian food."

Kate frowned, and my stomach hardened into lead. "I'm...not sure."

"About what?"

"About being seen together."

Nothing could soften those words. "Excuse me?"

"On the island, I mean." She sighed and planted her forehead against my chest. "I know this sounds horrible, but I really want to focus on getting this mall deal through the council. I don't want any one of those bastards being distracted by the fact that the mayor got herself a boyfriend."

I lifted her chin with my finger, torn between grinning and growling. "A boyfriend, huh?"

Oh, hell. That flush was intense.

"Well," she said, pulling away. "I mean… That's what people will think."

"What about you?" I pinned her with my gaze, moving close enough for our noses to touch. "What do you call me?"

"What do you want me to call you?"

"You're not ready to hear that yet, but boyfriend would work for now."

She sighed, her lips turning up into a cautious smile. "But you get it, right? My job? It wouldn't be forever—"

"I get it," I said, hating it, but understanding. "You need to push this deal through. I can be patient. I waited a fucking year for you—I can wait a few more days."

"Weeks."

I rolled her under me, sliding my cock through her wetness. "Don't push it, Kitten."

"Fuck." She sighed as I teased her clit. "You can't be ready again."

"Why not?"

"Because we just…finished."

"Oh, Kitten. I may not have that teenager stamina everyone seems to talk about, but I'm still in my prime." I slid into her bare, knowing I'd need to stop and grab a condom, wanting to tease her with just the tip for a few strokes first. "I've had to jack off three times in a row to thoughts of you when I only had your voice. Having your body under mine? Feeling your heat around me?" I pushed a little deeper, fighting every instinct I had and pulling out before I really screwed things up. "Being able to actually slide inside you and know what it's like to have your pussy all around my cock? I'll never get enough."

I reached for a condom, hoping I'd brought enough to sate my need for her tonight. I had a feeling things would be a little harder in the light of day, but that was okay. I had no trouble working for her attention. Days, maybe a couple of weeks, and we could act like any other couple. I could last that long.

I had to.

chapter eight

KATE

IT'D BEEN TWO long weeks since that night in the lighthouse…since Riley put every man I'd ever slept with to shame. What had been a once-weekly, thirty-minute talk had turned into hour-plus chats on the evenings Riley had off. On the days he was working, he'd text me the filthiest things… How he missed feeling me around him, missed the taste of me, was desperate to watch my pussy stretch around his cock.

The worst part was, I tended to be working when he'd text. I'd check my phone while I was meeting with councilpeople, thinking it was Lola updating me on the decided votes we were waiting on for the Huntley Group project. Instead, Riley's name would pop up, his dirty words on my screen, and I'd flush fifteen shades of red.

Like now.

You should wear the pink heels tonight. I know you hate walking in them, but I want them pressing into my shoulders while I suck on your clit, Kitten.

I glanced at my screen, a wave of heat washing over my body as I read his words.

"I'll be honest, Kate," Colin Huntley said, "you've got me very interested in whatever is on your phone."

I jumped, forgetting myself and the fact that I was supposed to be a professional, not the needy, sexual being I tended to revert to whenever Riley was around. "Sorry, Colin, I'm waiting for a message from Lola on Nicholson's vote."

"I take it that wasn't your assistant?"

With a laugh, I shook my head. "Definitely not." Before he could ask any more questions, I guided him through the abandoned mall and to the front doors. "If next week works for your schedule, we can set up a time, and I'll show you around Temperance Falls. Give you a peek into the town you're investing in."

He nodded, escorting me to my car. "I'll have Emery check my schedule and get back to you. Until then, keep working on Nicholson and see if you can bring him around. I'm not worried about him in a vote. What I *am* worried about is him swinging those on our side back to his."

"I'm working on it, Colin."

"I'm counting on you." He opened my car door for me, waiting for me to slide inside. "I hope you have a good evening with whoever is on the other end of that text." With a smile, he shut my door and strolled over to the car his driver had idling at the curb.

Jesus, that'd been close. I needed to be more careful while I was working. It wouldn't matter how often Riley and I ventured off the island for our dates if everything came to light because of some dirty texts.

My phone buzzed in my hand with an incoming call. Riley.

"Hello?"

"Don't tell me after everything I've said, *that* text was too far."

I laughed into the phone. "No. I was with Colin doing a walk-through at the old mall."

He grunted. "I don't like that guy."

"You don't have to like him. He's going to bring the island a shit-ton of money if—*when*—this deal goes through."

"Still don't like him," he grumbled.

I shook my head, rolling my eyes. "How's it at the firehouse?"

"It's been quiet today, though that means the time's been dragging. I think we washed the rig twice already. If the next few hours don't speed up, I'm going to go insane. I'd rather be with you than sitting here with all these guys."

I glanced at the time on my dashboard. "Well, you've only got three hours. We're meeting at Solstice in the city at seven, right?"

"Absolutely. Don't be late, now. I've been without you for two whole days."

"Poor baby. I'll be on time. I've got a few things to finish up at the office, then I'll head home to get ready. Traffic on the bridge shouldn't be too bad that time of night."

"You know, you could always let me be a gentleman and actually pick you up at your door."

I blew out a breath, knowing this had been coming. We'd gone out several times, always to the mainland, and before each date, he'd asked to come pick me up. And each time I'd told him the same thing. "I'm just not sure it's a good idea."

He sighed, an exhale so long, I could practically feel it through the phone. "Right. The mall deal. What's Nicholson's issue on this, anyway? Why can't he just vote for it and move on? We all know it's going through."

"Because he's a bastard who loves throwing roadblocks in my way. If I were lewd, I'd mention something about his resistance being a direct correlation to him compensating for what's lacking in his pants, but since I'm a professional, I'll keep my mouth shut."

"Aw, Kitten," Riley said, dropping his voice to the octave that never failed to make me wet. "You know I prefer you lewd. C'mon, give me a little something. What are you wearing over there all the way across the island?"

I shifted in the driver's seat, glancing down at myself. "My red suit. The one I wear the lacy black cami under."

"Hmmm. You've got the red heels on, too, don't you?"

"I do…" I bit my lip, remembering the last time

I'd had them on. "When I wore them for our date, you made me keep them on for you."

He groaned, and I imagined him gripping his cock through his work pants. "Trust me, I remember. Did you read my text?"

"Yes."

"You're gonna be a good girl and wear them for me, aren't you? I want to be the one to strip them off you. After they've left a few marks on my back."

"Such a bossy thing. Anything else I can wear… or not wear…for you?"

"I'll leave that up to you, Kitten. Though if you happened to forget to put on your panties, you might get a treat at the table. You know I can't resist you when I know you're bare under your little skirts."

———

At five to seven, I pulled into the darkened parking lot, sliding into the spot a couple down from Riley. Before I could do anything but turn off the car, he opened my door and helped me out, pulling me straight into his arms. He didn't wait a second before his mouth covered mine, his tongue sliding between my lips. I ran my hands over his shoulders, down his solid muscles, loving how huge he felt under my fingers. Loving how protected and safe he made me feel in his arms. Loving that I could let myself go enough around him even to appreciate such a thing. With his hands gripping my ass, he pressed me up against the side of my car, letting me feel exactly how much he wanted me.

God, two days without him was too long.

I panted when he pulled away, staring at his lips as I tried to catch my breath. "Well, that was quite a greeting."

"Missed you," he said as he nuzzled my neck. "Besides, how could I not greet you like that?" He pulled back, holding me out at arm's length as he looked me over from head to toe. "Damn, woman. You look good enough to eat."

"Maybe later." I grabbed his hand and pulled him along behind me, tossing him a smile over my shoulder.

"*Definitely* later."

Once inside Solstice, the host settled us at our table, a small round booth toward the back. Riley held out his arm for me to slide in first, then scooted around until he was next to me.

"Your waiter will be right with you," the host said before turning to leave.

"I've never been here." I glanced around, picking up my menu. "What made you choose this place?"

"They have amazing paella."

"Mmm...I love paella."

"I remember."

I jerked my head to him, my brows drawn together as I stared at him. "You do?"

"Of course. It was the first time you told me about your hatred of the pink shoes. You had that conference in Chicago and had been expecting boring, dry chicken, but they served paella instead. I've never heard someone so unhappy with their shoes but happy with their dinner at the same time."

I remembered that conference, remembered the pleasant surprise at having something delicious instead of the standard conference food. Remembered my talk with Riley that evening. I never imagined he would, too. "I can't believe you remember that. That was months ago."

He smiled, giving me a quick wink. "I remember everything. Like the fact that you love to pick your dessert first. They've got a chocolate fondue here I've heard is amazing. We can split it if you'd like."

I pressed a hand on his cheek, turning his head to mine so I could kiss him. Just because he was mine and he was amazing. "Since you remember everything, then you know chocolate fondue is one of my absolute favorites. So obviously, yes, we're going to share that."

"If there's any left over, we can take it home with us." He leaned over, his shoulder pressing into mine as he settled his lips against my ear. "I wouldn't mind licking chocolate off your nipples at some point. Could be fun."

God, the way this man spoke and then turned away as if he hadn't just suggested the filthiest things… He drove me crazy with want.

"Good evening," the waiter said, interrupting my thoughts. "Welcome to Solstice. May I offer you two something to drink? We have an excellent selection of wine."

Riley glanced over at me, his eyebrows raised. "Red?"

"Yes, please."

"A bottle of Pinot Noir, please."

"Of course, I'll bring that right out for you and let you take a look at the menu."

After the waiter had come back with our wine, pouring us each a glass, and taken our orders, he'd disappeared with a promise that the entrees would be out soon.

Riley placed his arm along the back of the booth, curving his body around mine as he scooted closer to me. "So, you wore one of your little skirts." With the arm resting along the back of the booth, he played with my hair, momentarily distracting me while his other hand reached for the hem of my skirt. "Did you forget something for me?"

I leaned my head back into his touch at the same time I settled my hand on top of his roaming one, stilling it on my upper thigh. "Maybe…"

He slid even closer, pressing his body right against mine and turning it toward me, nearly blocking out the restaurant behind him. And then he slipped his hand between my thighs, sliding it up under the hem of my skirt. "Maybe sounds promising."

"Riley," I hissed, darting my eyes around to the nearly full restaurant. "We can't do this out here."

Leaning in, he nuzzled my cheek and whispered, "Remember when I said your career would be safe with me by your side?" He waited for my nod before he continued with that hand—the one sent to drive me absolutely mad—sliding it straight up under my skirt. "I meant it. I'm watching out. I'll stop if we need to, but I can't wait another hour or more to get my hands on you. I've been dreaming about touching you for two damn days. But if you really want me to stop, I will. So what do you say…are you going to let me play with your pussy, baby?"

My heart nearly beat out of my chest, my nipples tightening at the idea that I was considering allowing him to do exactly what he wanted…in public where anyone could see. No, not *considering*. I was doing it. As much as he was craving touching me, I craved his touch in turn. I'd gone the year before with nothing but my hand, my fingers, my toys, and then suddenly two weeks with Riley, and I was desperate for him every minute of the day.

I spread my legs a little, enough to let him know I wanted to play his game. Enough so he could slip his hand higher until his fingers brushed against my bare pussy.

He hummed deep in his throat, his lips curving against my cheek. "You naughty girl, you. No panties tonight? I'm downright shocked." The sarcasm in his voice was heavy, but I didn't care. Not when he spread me wide with his thick fingers and pressed a fingertip to my clit.

I swallowed my moan, bit my lip to keep from screaming something wholly inappropriate. "You told me to leave them at home."

"I know, but you sometimes don't like to follow directions. You're my stubborn Kitten. Spread your legs a little more. Let me slip inside so I can get you good and wet."

"Riley…people are going to *see*," I hissed.

He pulled his hand out from between my legs, then plucked the cloth napkin off the table before dropping it in my lap. "They can't see past the tablecloth, but just in case, lay this over your lap for me."

He didn't wait for me to do as he'd said before he slid his hand between my legs, immediately seeking my pussy. Trailing his fingertips down one side and up the other, ghosting touches across my clit, he worked me up until I was desperate for more. No longer caring that we were in public, no longer panicked over the fact that we could be caught, I allowed my legs to fall open, allowed him better access.

And he took full advantage. With a soft hum in his throat, he worked a finger inside me, flicking my clit with his thumb, and I moaned under my breath.

"You gotta keep it down, Kitten. I can't make you come if I think you'll give us away. And I really want to make you come. I want to feel you come all over my hand."

"Oh my God, you can't say things like that and—" I broke off as he slid another finger inside me and pressed deep, biting my lip to stifle another moan. "I don't think I can be quiet."

"Then I guess I have to stop." He paused his movements, his fingers still filling me but not *doing* anything.

I gripped his wrist, shifting my hips forward, forcing his fingers deeper. "Please don't stop," I whispered.

"Naughty girl." He nuzzled my neck before pressing a kiss there. "Just don't scream."

With that, he added another finger, filling and stretching me. Making me buck my hips against him. Making me crave what he had in his pants instead of his fingers. Because as large as his hands were, as thick as those fingers he pumped inside me, they still paled in comparison to his cock.

"There it is. I feel you quivering. You're going to come on my fingers, aren't you? So naughty, here in a restaurant filled with people, and you're going to let me make you come right on my hand." He continued the soft strokes of my hair with his other hand, such a filthy contradiction to the lewd things he was doing under the tablecloth. "Hurry up, baby, the waiter's coming."

Oh God. The thought that I had seconds before someone was upon us sent me over the edge, Riley's fingers deep inside me as I tightened around him while his thumb circled my clit.

"Fuck, I feel you coming on me. Kiss me, Kate. Give me your lips, too."

I did as he asked, turning my head toward him and letting my eyes fall closed as he took my mouth in a kiss. So soft and sweet, just the barest brush of his tongue against mine even as he had three fingers thrust deep in my pussy.

"Ah, yes, here we are," the waiter said, placing our plates in front of us. "The paella for the lady, and the braised short ribs for the gentleman. Anything else right away?"

"A glass of water for my girlfriend, please," Riley said, still curving his body around mine. "She's feeling a little flushed."

"Of course, I'll be right back with that."

As soon as the waiter was out of hearing range, I slapped Riley on the shoulder. "Oh my God. I can't believe you just said that."

He grinned before leaning in to brush his lips against my cheek. "I'm sorry, but your chest is bright pink. You might've masked the sounds of you coming, but you can't hide the way you flush."

Slipping his fingers from inside me, he grabbed the napkin in my lap and wiped his hand, then settled it across his thighs.

"You don't want to go wash up?" I asked as I took my first bite, not able to help myself.

He shrugged as he topped off my glass of wine. "I don't really see the point. In an hour or so, my mouth is gonna be where my fingers just were." He only smirked at my gasp. "How's your paella?"

God, this man. I stared at him, shaking my head. "I swear, how you can go from absolutely *filthy* to perfect gentleman in the span of two seconds is baffling."

He leaned over and pressed a kiss to my temple. "You bring out the best and worst in me. Now, let's get you fed. I've got plans for you tonight that will require lots of energy."

"I bet. And it's delicious, thanks for asking. How's yours?"

He chewed thoughtfully, then shook his head. "Not as good as your pussy, but I can fill up on that later."

"See?" I pointed my fork toward him. "*Filthy.*"

Grinning, he speared another bite of his meal. "You never did tell me how the meeting went with Huntley today."

"It went well, I think. Colin's itching to get started on the space. We're both a little worried about Nicholson, so he wants me to keep on top of it."

"Yeah, I bet he wants you on top of things." He waved me off when I glared at him. "Kidding. Sort of. Sorry, I just…it took me a long time to actually make a move. I don't want to think about someone else trying to come between us."

"Riley…" I breathed, brushing my hand down his cheek. "You're worried about nothing. First of all, every interaction I've had with him has been nothing but professional. Second, in case it wasn't clear, I'm sort of smitten with someone else."

"If it's the someone I hope it is, he's sort of smitten with you, too."

I couldn't contain my smile, and I felt like a foolish schoolgirl because of it. Even so, I leaned over and pressed my lips to his.

I wasn't sure there was anything better than good food and good conversation all with a good—no, amazing—man. I never wanted the night to end.

Once we'd finished eating and placed our silverware across our empty dishes, the waiter appeared. "Let me clear these plates for you. Here's the dessert menu for you to look over. I'll be back in a couple minutes."

"Fondue, baby?" Riley asked after the waiter slipped away.

"Oh my God, I'm so full. I ate that entire bowl of

paella!" I leaned against the booth, resting my hand on my stomach. "I don't think I can eat another bite."

"Then we're getting it to go. I wasn't kidding when I said I wanted to lick it off you later."

"There's no place to clean up at the lighthouse, though."

"Yeah, we'll have to be careful."

"I'm not sure how careful we can be with melted chocolate. We're going to be a mess."

"I'll give you my shirt to wear home if you're sticky." He shrugged, topping off my glass with the rest of the wine. "It's no problem. I don't want you to ruin your clothes."

I looked at him—really looked. He was overwhelming, this monster of a man, tall and broad with muscles for days, but he was a gentle giant. At least with me. At least in the ways that mattered. True, in the bedroom, he handled me like a man possessed, but everywhere else, he treated me like a queen. Deferred to me on the things that were important to me, like when it came to anything that could harm my career.

He'd been so patient these past two weeks as we'd had hidden dates off the island, punctuated by clandestine trysts in an abandoned lighthouse. I loved that he'd been willing to do that for me, despite knowing how desperately he wanted to be at my side on the island. He'd told me time and time again how he couldn't wait until he could stroll down Main Street with my hand in his, so everyone would know he was mine.

And he was… Mine. Just as I was his. It didn't make sense, *we* didn't make sense, but my heart didn't care.

We couldn't venture out in the open yet, not completely. But I could give him something. I could share a part of myself with him, show him how much he meant to me—how much what we had meant to me.

"We could…" I cleared my throat, smoothing my napkin across my lap. "We could go back to my place. If you promised to park a few houses down."

He snapped his head in my direction. "Are you serious?"

I cringed. "I'm sorry, I know that's a shitty thing for me to ask—for you to park down the street—but I—"

"Sir," Riley called to our waiter as he passed by, then pulled out his wallet and handed the waiter his credit card. "We're going to need the chocolate fondue to go and for you to process our bill. We have an emergency."

"Of course, I'll request a rush on that, and I'll be right back with your check." The waiter hurried off without another word.

"Riley—"

He gripped my face and pulled me in for a kiss, sealing his lips over mine. Pulling back, he ran his thumbs over my cheeks, staring into my eyes. "Every week for the last year, at some point I'd tell you to lie back on your bed. My imagination is good, Kate—it's real fucking good—and these dates at the lighthouse have been amazing. But I want to see you on that bed. I want that fantasy realized."

I wanted that, too. Hadn't even realized how desperately until he'd said that. I bit my lip to hide my smile and closed the short distance between us to press our lips together once more. "Okay."

chapter nine

IF KATE MINDED the fact that I was basically humping her ass as she unlocked her back door, she certainly didn't show it.

"That's not the handle, Kitten." I kissed down the length of her neck, rubbing against where she'd slipped her hand between us. Bonus that I got a solid press against her ass while doing so. "You'd better get the door opened, or we're going to give the neighborhood a show."

She laughed and removed her hand, which only made me crave her more. It had been a quiet and lonely drive from the restaurant to her block, and I was ready to pin her to the damn door and strip her right there. I wanted to be inside her in the worst way.

But when she finally opened the door and stepped inside, the throb of lust I'd been feeling since she'd invited me back to her place faded into something quieter. Calmer.

This was an important moment… Kate had allowed me into her home.

I crossed the threshold and froze, trying to take in every detail. She was halfway across the room before she realized I'd barely taken a step inside.

"You coming?"

I nodded and licked my lips, unable to keep my eyes on hers. Too busy trying to learn everything I could in those precious few seconds. The place smelled like her, the gentle, flowery perfume she wore lingering on the air. It looked like her, too. Light colors, dark accent pieces, and splashes of color that seemed purposefully placed. Nothing professionally decorated about the space, more natural. Lived in. There was a small stack of books on the table by the fireplace and a single coffee cup next to the sink. Signs of life. Signs of *her* life.

"Riley?"

"It's you."

"Pardon?"

I took a good look around before shrugging. "This. It's you. I can see you here."

"Well, yeah. I mean, I've lived here a few years—"

I was across the room and on her before she could finish her sentence, kissing her deeply and pulling her body into mine for one long, slow minute.

"Thank you," I said when I finally released her. "I know what a big deal it is to let me into this space."

"You're welcome." She ran a hand over my cheek,

looking up at me with emotions she hadn't yet put into words. "Thank you for being patient with me."

As if I had any other choice. I would've stopped the world from spinning if she'd asked me to. "I'd wait forever if I had to, though I'd probably complain about it. A lot."

She laughed, tossing her head back, gripping my shoulders. So fucking gorgeous. "Yes, you would. You've certainly proven that."

"It's not something I can control, Kitten. I see you, I want you. All the time. Period. Now…I want to see the rest of this place. Show me you, Kate."

And she did. From soft, comfortable couches to the bookshelves practically groaning under the weight on them, every piece spoke of the woman at my side. She took me from room to room, showing me bits and pieces of herself as we toured her home. A graduation picture, a framed degree, a stack of papers in some random corner…memories of her life before me, her path to the mayorship. Her world. It was a window into her past and a base of her present. I loved it.

"Saved the best for last…" Kate stood to one side, looking almost nervous as I stepped into her most private space.

I inspected her bedroom, letting the details soak in. Taking in the simple, quiet style of the place. The feminine touches that added a little softness. "It suits you."

Her head cock only made me grin. "I'm really not sure if I should take that as a compliment or not."

"Always a compliment." I held out a hand, needing her beside me. Wanting to feel her body against mine. "Come here, baby."

She lagged for just a second before walking over to me, her steps slow and measured. Her eyes on mine the entire way. Wary but wanting. When she finally reached me, I wrapped my arms around her and tugged her against my chest.

"Tonight is different," I murmured, rocking her gently from side to side. "I don't want hard and fast right now. I don't want to pull out every filthy sentence I know to get you off. I just want you and me in that big-ass bed of yours. Let me love you, Kate."

KATE

I stared into Riley's eyes, his words of love settling over me like a warm blanket. I didn't know if he meant them at face value, or if he was simply using the phrase offhandedly. Regardless, I couldn't stop my heart from stuttering.

He cupped my face, brushing his thumbs over my cheeks. Came closer until his breath ghosted over my lips. "I do, you know. You may not be ready to hear it yet, but I love you, Kate."

His words knocked me off-balance, and I gripped his wrists, certain if he hadn't been holding me, I would've crumpled right to the ground. I shook my head, searching his eyes. "We don't make sense, Riley. Everything about this—us—is crazy."

He pressed a soft kiss on my lips. "Why do we need to make sense? Why can't we just be happy together? Is that so hard to do?"

"What if…" I stopped. Swallowed. Closed my eyes. I wasn't naturally a nervous person—I *couldn't* be in my position—but right then, my nerves were eating me alive, a dozen different *what-if* scenarios driving me crazy.

I loved Riley, *had* loved him for a long time— there was no denying the fall had been slow and pure… There was also no denying it had happened months ago when he'd been just Banner to me. When I'd only known him as a voice of comfort, of support.

But sometimes love wasn't enough.

I'd already lived through my twenties and thirties, and he hadn't had the chance. I didn't want to keep him from any of it. I didn't want my presence in his life to be a hindrance.

I curled my fingers tighter on his wrists. "What if being with me keeps you from living your life? You're only twenty-six. You still have so much to see…to do."

"And we can do it all together. You're not holding me back, baby. Don't you see that? You make everything worthwhile. Whatever comes at us, I want to handle it together."

I stared at him, my nails no doubt leaving crescent shapes on his skin. Though I'd tried to ignore the thought that he might come to resent me—or worse, to regret what we had—it was still there. Flashing like a neon sign in my mind, refusing to be silent.

Closing my eyes, I whispered, "I'm just so worried you're going to regret us."

He pulled me closer, pressing tender kisses on my closed lids. Then he enveloped me in his arms, and suddenly the whispers quieted. The worries faded to the background. In Riley's arms, everything felt right.

Lips brushing my ear, he said, "Regret what? Spending my life with an intelligent, beautiful woman who sure as fuck doesn't *need* me standing beside her?" He pulled back to cup my face again. "Not going to happen."

One thing I loved about Riley was how he wore his emotions on his sleeve. There was no hiding with him—what you saw was what you got. On a normal day, it was refreshing. Right then, it was beyond refreshing. It was *reassuring.* There was no second-guessing on my part. I could read the sincerity in his eyes. Could see every ounce of it in the way he looked at me.

I wrapped my arms around his neck and pressed up on my toes, resting my lips against his. "I love you, too."

His eyes flared, his hands slipping down to cup my ass as he hauled me up against him. And then his mouth was hungry on mine.

"Christ, Kitten…hearing you say that drives me fucking crazy." He tossed me onto the bed and climbed on top, caging me in. "I'm gonna love you so hard tonight. Gonna kiss every inch of you, then find all the places I missed and love them with my tongue."

We stripped each other slowly, sliding our hands along one another as we peeled off articles of clothing, tossing them in different directions. Until, finally, we were both bare.

He did exactly as he'd said, first flipping me on my stomach so he could kiss down my spine, along my shoulder blades, the backs of my knees, and every inch in between. As if I weren't writhing and needy for him, he turned me over and repeated the entire process all over again, incorporating his tongue into the mix just to tease me more.

"Riley." I panted, grappling at his shoulders as he settled between my legs.

"Yeah?" He flicked his tongue against my clit in a mindless sort of way, causing my hips to jerk. "You need something?"

I moaned when he did it again, this time with more purpose, sucking my clit into his mouth. "Please… Come up here. I need you inside me."

He groaned against me, the vibration on my clit pushing me that much closer to the edge. With one last lick through my slit, he rose above me, resting his arms on either side of my head. "I can't refuse you anything."

Leaning over, he grabbed his pants from the floor, pulling out a condom before rolling it down his length. God, what the sight of him did to me— his huge fist gripping his cock, giving it a little tug as he protected us both. I wanted to climb him like a tree, cling to his mountain-man shoulders, and never let go.

He sat back on his heels, running his hand from my knee down my inner thigh, not stopping until he rubbed soft, slow circles around my clit. "You wanna ride me? Let me look at you for a while?"

I arched my back, pushing harder against him. Needing more. Closing my eyes, I shook my head against the pillow and reached for him. "Not yet… just want to feel you."

He crawled over me, brushing openmouthed kisses against my skin along the way. Sucked a nipple into his mouth, letting it go with a pop, his lips spreading in a smile when I moaned and arched against him. "You know I'd give you anything. You want to feel me? You mean your greedy little pussy wants my cock? I'll give that to you. I'll always give you what you need." He gripped his heavy erection and ran it through where I was an absolute mess of wetness for him, making me mindless with need. Then he put me out of my misery and slowly pushed inside.

I bit my lip, feeling the delicious pleasure-pain of him stretching me wide to accommodate his size. Riley was a beast of a man, tall and broad, and he had a cock to match. Being with him never got old, never got any less intense. Every time was like the first. "Riley…"

He groaned, holding himself over me as he looked down to where I was spread wide around him, opening to take every inch of his cock. "Fuck, Kitten, it's like coming home every time I slide into your pussy."

Settling on his forearms, he covered me, let me feel his body along the length of mine but careful to keep the majority of his weight off me. He started an unhurried, steady rhythm, pulling back in a slow retreat, only to snap forward, sliding deep as he rotated his hips against me. No matter how we did this—fast, slow, rushed, languid—he never failed to make my body sing. From the start, I was nearly ready to go off. The pressure every drive into me put on my clit was just enough to keep me on edge, but not enough to push me over. And he fucking knew it.

"Please, please, I need more. Riley—" I broke off when he reached behind him and unhooked my ankles from around his hips, lifting one until it rested on his shoulder. Then he once again did his slow retreat, deep thrust, and I saw stars. "Holy *shit*."

"You feel that? How can this be crazy? How could I ever regret how I feel about you? Just trust me, Kate. Let me love you, and everything will be okay. I promise."

I bit my lip and nodded, trusting him to treat my heart as well as he'd proven with my body. Maybe I was worried for nothing. Maybe my fears were unfounded. Maybe a relationship really could be this easy—no complications, no hidden agendas, no burning resentment. Just two people, connecting with each other, supporting each other…loving each other.

I ran my hands over every inch of him that I could

reach, totally and completely lost to Riley—how he took my mouth in a consuming kiss, whispered dirty things in my ear, leaned down and tugged a nipple between his teeth only to turn his head and press his lips softly against my ankle. Dirty and sweet. Slow and hard. The most beautiful contradiction.

"Fuck, Kitten. I could do this every day. Could slide deep inside your pussy and make you scream every fucking morning before you even rolled out of bed. That's not crazy. That's heaven."

"I want that. I want you—" I gasped and arched against him when he dropped a hand between us, his thumb seeking out my clit. "Oh, yes, right there."

"I know, baby. I know." He leaned down, sucking my bottom lip into his mouth as I panted toward the ceiling. "I know all your spots, don't I? Know how to get you off. Are you ready to come?"

"Oh my God, yes."

"Then hold on, Kitten."

He dug his fingers into my leg, my ankle still propped on his shoulder, and snapped his hips forward, beginning a fast and frenzied pace. "I know how to take care of this tight little pussy, don't I? Know exactly what it needs."

I clawed at his arms, desperate to come. Desperate to make *him* come. Wanting nothing more than to feel him come apart because of me.

He groaned and dropped his head, looking at where we were connected. "That's it. Your thighs are quivering. You're about to come all over my cock, aren't you? I wanna hear those words when you come. Give them to me."

He could've been talking about a hundred different things, but when he lifted his head and locked his eyes on mine, I knew exactly what he meant…exactly what he wanted to hear.

With fast flicks to my clit, he pushed me right over the edge, my body arching in bliss. I dug my nails into his biceps and pressed my head back into the pillow. "Love you, love you, Riley. Oh God, I'm coming."

"That's my girl." He groaned as I pulsed around him, thrusting twice more before he pushed deep and let himself go, moaning my name through his release. "Christ, I love you. How could anything about this be bad? You're perfect, *we're* perfect."

He smoothed his hand up my leg, lifting my calf off his shoulder and letting it fall to his side. With gentle hands, he kneaded my tense muscles as he settled on top of me. "You believe me now?"

I welcomed the comforting pressure of his weight against me, loving how cared for and safe it made me feel, his words providing that same comfort to my heart. "I believe you."

"Good." He gripped the base of his cock to hold the condom in place and pulled out of me, both of us groaning at the loss. "Because I've got a lot more loving to do tonight. We're gonna christen every damn room of this house before I leave. I don't want you going anywhere without thinking about how good I loved you in each and every one."

chapter ten

RILEY

"YO, NASH. Captain's called a meeting in thirty."

I waved a hand at Big John and kept walking. "Showering. Be down in a bit."

Being back at work after two whole days doing nothing but talking to Kate, taking care of Kate, and fucking Kate was a real piece of shit. I'd been at the firehouse for forty-three hours already and had done nothing but sit around watching television and texting her. I needed to get my head clear in case a call came in. I couldn't be distracted in a fire.

The bathroom was thankfully empty, so I headed down to one of the shower stalls at the end. A quick wash and a solid jack, and I'd be fine. It wasn't the first time I'd had to take matters into my own hand at the firehouse because of thoughts of Kate. It certainly wouldn't be the last.

I stood under the steaming water and soaped up, fast as hell with every action. Until I got to my cock. I slowed then, took my time. Gave my dick every bit of the attention he needed right then as I let my mind wander back to Kate. And Kate's bedroom.

With a couple of twists to the tip, I remembered how her pale skin looked against the dark bedding, how she'd seemed to glow like a fucking angel as she'd sprawled naked on the bed for me. And pink? Yeah, there had been pink. Small bits, accents, practically hidden—just like my favorite bits of Kate's pink.

I'd eaten her pussy eight times in two days—on the bed, with her at her desk in her home office, on the kitchen counter, in the shower. Location didn't matter. If she let me between her thighs, I was a man obsessed.

And the fucking. Good goddamn, I actually ached from it. And not in my cock. My back hurt, my hips were sore, and I was pretty sure I could skip leg day that week, seeing as how I could barely walk the night before.

I slid my hand up and down my length faster, unable not to. Picturing every naughty thing we'd done that weekend. A tingle started in my balls and quickly spread to my spine, all thoughts of anything other than Kate full-on naked and spread in front of me disappearing. Just a few more…a little tighter. Fuck, it'd feel so much better if she had her hand on me, would be a fucking treat if she'd wrap her lips around me the way she had this weekend. On her knees in the shower, the water hitting my back just as it was now. The warmth of her mouth as she took me in, as she swallowed me down, as she grabbed my ass and looked up at me with those huge blue eyes before she licked—

"Fuck," I groaned, unable to hold on another second. I came with a grunt, keeping my hand running from base to tip to extend that wave. To snag every ounce of pleasure.

It wasn't as good as being with Kate, but it'd have to do.

Once I dried off and re-dressed, I headed downstairs. Ready for this meeting the captain had called. Probably some task he wanted us to do, some extra work to keep us busy. I was all for staying busy. The more I worked, the faster the time went. Bring on the honey-do lists.

I grabbed my phone on the way past my sleeping area, frowning when I saw I had no alerts. Kate hadn't texted me back all morning. I knew she had a busy day, but that was unlike her. I sent her one last *everything okay?* text before hitting the stairs and slipping into the garage where the captain was just getting started.

"We have a couple of visitors coming in just a few minutes." The captain nodded to his lieutenant, who pressed the buttons to open the bay doors. "I'll be giving them a tour, and I'd like a couple of guys to accompany us in case they have questions." He scowled when the entire crew groaned. "Yeah, yeah—no one wants to do the fucking job. Trust me, you're going to want to in about five minutes when they come inside. So shore up and get ready. And do *not* forget the rules: be polite, be respectful, and for God's sake, don't fucking swear when talking to any of them."

I snuck up beside Big John, trying to see who the hell was coming. "Is he fucking serious?"

"A-fucking-pparently." John stretched and groaned. "I hate when my forty-eight off fall on the weekend."

"Said no one ever."

"Nah, man. I'm serious. I always feel this need to accomplish shit instead of just fucking around at home."

"Did you actually leave this house this weekend?"

"I worked at the lighthouse, unlike some people." John's jaw clicked, and a muscle at the corner jumped. "Jackson said you haven't been taking a lot of shifts lately. Something up?"

Fuck. I really had been neglecting my work at the construction site. I needed to get in touch with Jackson and let him know I wasn't bailing on him. I'd been so wrapped up in seeing Kate whenever I could that I'd slacked. Unfortunately, I still couldn't tell anyone that particular reason. Not even Big John or Jackson. A fact that made my stomach grow heavy. "Not really, I've just been busy."

Big John gave me a look that said he didn't buy my bullshit. "Busy, huh? Sounds like—"

"Gentlemen," the captain said, loud enough to grab all our attention, which saved me from having to explain anything more to Big John. "Please welcome Mr. Colin Huntley, CEO of Huntley Group, Mayor Kate Briscoe, and someone we should all know considering she's been running around the neighborhood her entire life, Miss Emery Collins, to the firehouse."

My entire world went sideways. Kate, looking fucking stunning in a tan suit with a light pink scarf around her neck, stood in my firehouse. So did Emery, whose dad was the local police chief. The girl had grown up, though she didn't hold a candle to my Kate. Still, the whole crowd of men around me seemed to tense up at the presence of the visitors, specifically the women.

Including the man at my side.

"Motherfucker," John breathed, the words almost too quiet for me to hear. I glanced at him, following his gaze to the front. To...Emery?

"Something you need to tell me?" I raised my eyebrows, nodding my head in the direction of the girl half this firehouse probably saw as a little sister. John had more reason than any of them—his mom and Emery's dad had married a few years back.

"You first." John brought his eyes to meet mine, nodding toward Kate. "Or were you excited by the guy in the suit?"

Busted. I kept my voice low, trying not to let anyone overhear. "I ain't talking yet. I can't."

"Ditto, man." With a pat to my shoulder, John turned and stormed off, disappearing up the back stairs that led to the living areas.

I had no time to worry about him, though. No

time to consider that someone on the island knew my secret, especially considering I didn't care if it got out or not. I was too caught up with Kate. Seeing her smile, watching her interact with the crew. Seeing how that Colin guy kept a hand on the small of her back to lead her around.

Motherfucker was right.

"We'll head upstairs first, let you see where the team lives while they're here. You may not know this, but our firemen and EMTs work forty-eight-hour shifts. That means they…"

I filtered out the captain's babble, sneaking up behind Kate as she headed for the stairs. The woman was in some serious heels, and the stairs were tight. No way was I letting her fall. She glanced over her shoulder as she hit the middle landing, one side of her mouth turning up into her real smile. Subtle, but I'd take it.

"Kate." Colin held out his hand when he reached the top, grabbing my girl and pulling her beside him. I was going to break that fucker's fingers if he didn't learn to keep his hands to himself, but Kate seemed okay with it. Well, not okay—accepting. Maybe he always treated her like this. A thought that had my blood boiling. Kate was mine, and no other man should've felt they could touch her.

But there was shit-all I could do about him.

The captain walked everyone through the bunk rooms and the kitchen, telling stories of pranks and family-style meals, of middle of the night calls and parties we threw for things like engagements and new babies. He was pushing that wholesome, family vibe—something almost comical considering I'd jacked off just minutes before in the shower room.

"We'll head downstairs to check out the operations room," the captain said as we circled back toward the stairs.

"No fire pole?" Colin asked, and I almost rolled my eyes. Of course there was.

The captain laughed and answered with something about back rooms and forgetfulness before leading everyone toward the fire pole at the opposite end of the floor. If this was like any other tour, they'd spend a good ten minutes there with people sliding down the pole just for fun. Kate had separated herself to the back of the group, her phone in her hand and a serious look on her face.

Time to act.

As the group filed to the right, I snagged Kate's arm and pulled her into the shower room.

"Riley, what—"

I silenced her with a kiss, unable to wait a second more. She groaned and opened her mouth for me, letting me slip my tongue against hers. Clinging to my shoulders as she rose onto the balls of her feet to try to move closer. Game on.

"You weren't answering my texts," I whispered as I directed her farther into the space.

"I was with Colin. He's already commented on my reaction while reading texts. I didn't want him to actually see what you'd written."

I grunted, pushing Kate against the wall separating

two showers. The one I'd left shortly before—still wet—and a dry one. "Those words are for you alone, Kitten."

She tried to pull me closer, to kiss me again. Needy little thing. "I know. That's why I didn't read them in front of him."

I leaned down and nipped her neck, needing to steal a taste. "Know what I was doing right before you got here?"

"What?"

"Jacking off in this shower." I nearly grinned at her little gasp. "See how wet it is in there? That's because of me. Because I couldn't get my mind off our weekend together. Fuck, Kitten—do you know how hot the thought of you on your knees made me?"

She dropped her hands to my crotch and ran her fingers over where I was already so hard and aching for her. "I can't wait for you to finish your shift."

Aw, that was cute. She really had no clue what I had planned. "Yeah, neither can I. But you don't get me right after my shift, remember? It's family night at the Nash house. You have to be patient."

Her frustrated groan did nothing to calm me down.

"Yeah, I have no patience when it comes to you, either." I lifted her and spread her legs around me, forcing her tight skirt up her thighs. She gasped and looked around, almost panicked, but I shushed her as I moved to balance her on my left arm.

"Don't worry, Kitten. There's no way any of the crew is going to come in here when there are VIPs in the building."

"Someone will notice I'm gone."

"I guess we'd better hurry, then." I slid my right hand up under her skirt and ran a knuckle over her clit, loving the way her entire body seemed to pulse at my touch, the way she bit into her bottom lip to keep from moaning. My girl loved the way I played with her pussy, but this wasn't a time for slow or fun. I needed to prove a point, to claim her and erase the image of the suited-up fucker putting his hand on my girl, and to get her off as only I could. Nothing else mattered.

I leaned in, sliding a finger inside her and pumping it a few times before adding a second. And when I'd worked those two as deep as I could, when I curled them in that way that made her shake and groan, when I pressed my thumb against her clit and began to circle it, I whispered one last instruction. "Try not to scream."

I took her mouth in a kiss that set me on fire, using every trick I'd learned to get her off fast. Fingers curled, stroking, pressing hard on her clit, I multitasked like a fucking champion. Her legs trembled, and her entire body writhed against my hand, telling me all I needed to know. She was close already. She just needed a little more. An extra push.

I slipped a third finger inside her and doubled down on the pressure to her clit. Jackpot. Kate jerked and bit her lip hard, her pussy milking my fingers as she came in my arms. As she clung to my shoulders and held back the moan I knew she wanted to release.

A soft squeak of a shoe on tile distracted me,

making me look up and away from Kate. Big John stood just inside the doorway that led to the sleeping quarters, his eyes on mine. His face unreadable. I didn't move, didn't really breathe until he nodded his head once and turned to leave.

Yeah, there was no hiding Kate and me anymore. At least, not from John.

Kate hummed and dropped her forehead to my shoulder, completely oblivious to our witness. Which was fine with me.

"Good girl," I whispered, refocusing on her, keeping my fingers deep inside her as she softened and relaxed. "Was that what you needed, Kitten?"

"Oh God, yes," she said with a sigh.

I couldn't help it—I laughed. "I think I'm rubbing off on you."

She laid her head against my chest as I lowered her to her feet. "Probably." When she finally looked up at me, she smiled, relaxed and radiant. Perfect. "I have to go back to work."

"I know." I grabbed her by the ass and tugged her closer. "See you later?"

"Absolutely."

I walked her down the stairs, slipping into the crowd in the equipment room without anyone noticing. They noticed Kate, though. How could they not?

"Mayor Briscoe," that bastard Colin called. "We thought we'd lost you."

"I apologize. I needed to use the restroom." She practically glided to the front of the room, her head high and her steps sure. My confident Kitten. "What did I miss?"

Big John slid into place beside me, his shoulders back and his eyes on Kate. "Riley."

As much as I trusted the man, Kate didn't. And as much as I hated having to hide, I needed to protect her. "Do we have anything to worry about, John?"

He huffed a laugh, practically spinning on the spot when a smiling Emery came dancing into the room. "Not a thing. I've got your six."

"Thanks." I raised my chin toward where he was staring, toward Emery. "And I've got yours. When you're ready."

"Never gonna happen," he grumbled before stomping back down the hallway and toward the rig bays.

The tour wrapped up soon after that, but I stuck around. One, because Kate was still there talking to the captain, but two, because that Colin fucker was there as well.

"Thank you all for your time," Kate said as the group readied to leave. "I hope you know this project will not only bring affordable housing to our community, but also jobs and growth. We appreciate your support as we update Temperance Falls for a new generation of residents."

She shook the captain's hand, stepping back to allow Colin to do the same before she started a conversation with Emery and the chief.

I spotted my opportunity and stepped into Colin's space. "Firefighter Nash. Thank you for taking the time to stop by today."

The guy looked slightly confused and disinterested. "Yes, well…thank you all for being so hospitable."

I reached out, offering my hand. Meeting Kate's worried eyes as my fingers gripped his.

My fingers that were still damp from being inside Kate's pussy.

His smile faltered when I grabbed his hand, falling completely when I squeezed way too hard for polite company.

"A real man doesn't need to pull a woman along with him," I murmured as I edged a step closer. "You might want to learn to keep your motherfucking hands to yourself."

With that, I pushed him back just enough to break the handshake. His brows drew down, his eyes examining me. Kate's were wide, almost fearful. I shot her a quick smile and turned, heading back to the equipment room to inventory my kit. I'd made my point. She was mine, and he needed to back off. No business deal was worth losing her.

chapter eleven

KATE

NORMALLY A RILEY-INDUCED orgasm left me boneless. Sated. Carefree. Now, though, as I walked with Colin to city hall, I was on edge. Part adrenaline still coursing through my veins over the excitement that Riley and I could've gotten caught, and part fear over what would've happened if we had been.

I didn't even want to think about the fallout had we been found. Had the captain or any one of the firefighters—or, God forbid, Colin—come into the shower room while Riley'd had me pushed up against the wall, his fingers working inside me… I couldn't even consider it. In my time as mayor, I'd had to talk my way out of a lot of sticky situations, but even I wouldn't have been able to get us out of that.

The what-ifs of the scenario were terrifying, especially knowing Colin had been who knew how close while it'd happened. What was more terrifying was the fact that I'd let Riley do it. With little hesitation. Okay…with *no* hesitation. My entire career hinged on this mall deal I was finessing, and one wrong step with Huntley was a step I couldn't afford to take. And I'd just let my boyfriend finger me while I was supposed to be working because Riley managed to make me forget everything but him.

"I appreciate your scheduling this tour for me today, Kate," Colin said, pulling me from my thoughts.

I startled, glancing over and attempting to paste on a convincing smile even as my heart nearly beat out of my chest. "Oh, it was no trouble at all."

The adrenaline and fear racing through me were understandable. Excusable. What *wasn't* either of those things was the fact that my panties were still wet, my nipples tight, and the thoughts currently consuming me were focused on the memory of the look in Riley's eyes as he'd shook Colin's hand. It'd been some macho bullshit, a *who has the biggest dick* competition to which I was no stranger in the political arena. But Riley had taken it a step further. He'd radiated smugness. I had no idea what he'd said to Colin, but Riley's body language couldn't have been any plainer to read than if he'd been a book—he'd staked his claim on me.

I hated how much I loved it.

"I always knew Temperance Falls was a great place, but this showcased that even more thoroughly." Colin opened the door to city hall, holding it for me as he ushered me ahead of him.

"That's what I was hoping," I said, forcing myself

to get under control. I was a fully grown woman with a job to do, and I couldn't let Riley distract me from it. "I'm glad it worked for your schedule to come out here. I know you're busy."

"Right now, this is my top priority. I want to make sure everything's in place to make the transition run like a well-oiled machine." He followed me to my outer office, nodding at Lola when she said hello, and strolling straight into my inner office.

"A few messages came in for you while you were gone, Mayor Briscoe." Lola handed me a couple slips of paper. "I'll hold your calls until your meeting is finished."

"Thank you, Lola." I collected the messages and slipped into my office, shutting the door behind me.

Colin stood by the large window against the far wall, turning around to face me as I came inside, the look on his face unreadable.

"You mentioned wanting to make sure things run smoothly for this acquisition," I said, taking a seat behind my desk, "but I think we're on track. I spoke with Nicholson a couple days ago, and I'm confident I'm starting to warm him to the idea of this bringing revenue to the island."

"I'm glad to hear that." He slipped his hands into the pockets of his suit pants, eyes never leaving mine. "And what about you, Kate?"

"Me?" I asked, brow furrowed.

"Are you focused on this deal?" He settled in a chair in front of my desk, reclining back as he rested his ankle on his opposite knee—the picture of ease.

"Of course. It's number one on my list and has been for—"

"Are you seeing anyone right now?"

I jerked my head away, blinking in disbelief. While in this position of authority, I'd had my share of men hitting on me—mostly those who thought they could get something out of the situation. But it'd never been so blatant. And Colin's polished exterior alluded to the fact that he'd be a bit more refined in his approach, which only threw me more.

I couldn't deny he was handsome in that perfect sort of way. His dark hair was always in place, and he rocked his expensive, tailored suits which were hiding what was no doubt the kind of body one achieved from spending five days a week at the gym. Rigid. Disciplined. But he was the complete opposite of Riley—dark to Riley's light, smooth to his rough. The opposite of everything currently holding my attraction.

"Ex-excuse me?"

He held up his hand in surrender. "Relax. I'm not hitting on you. I apologize for the brusque way I'm bringing this up, but I'm a straight shooter, Kate. And considering the business relationship we're embarking on, I think it's something I deserve to know."

"Working relationship or not, I'm not sure how it's any of your business." I swallowed, resting my arms on my desk and leaning toward him. Exuding a confidence I didn't feel.

"Consider it a professional courtesy to me. I'm intent on investing almost a billion dollars into your picturesque little island here. And I tend to get a bit twitchy with that much money on the line."

I could see his point. The amount he was putting into this island was more than I'd see in ten lifetimes. I could understand why he'd want to make sure everything was running smoothly, that nothing would get in the way of the deal. And even if I mentioned I was seeing someone, that didn't mean I had to divulge *who* it was.

I sighed. "Yes, I am. However, it's not known around the island. I keep my private life private."

He studied me, his eyes boring into mine. I could practically see the wheels spinning in his mind. "If that's really what you're intending, I think a bit more discretion may be in order."

"I'm not sure what you mean." I forced the words out, even though my throat had gone tight with nerves.

Somehow, Colin had found out about Riley and me. I was sure of it. It couldn't have been coincidence that this conversation came up immediately after leaving the firehouse. Oh God…had he seen Riley snag me away from the group while on the tour? Had he happened upon us in the shower room, and I'd been too far into the throes of orgasm to even notice? I blanched at the thought, my heart racing.

"I mean, your…boyfriend?" he asked, as if unsure the word to use. "The big guy at the firehouse, right?"

I couldn't answer…could only stare at him. But I didn't need to say a thing—he took my silence as acquiescence.

He nodded once and smoothed a hand down his striped tie. "Thought so. *You* might be trying to keep it under wraps, but is he aware of that?"

I swallowed. "Yes…"

Cocking a brow, he stared at me in silence for long moments before clearing his throat. "The two of you may want to have a chat. Because he couldn't have been clearer to me than if he'd pissed a circle around you."

"Oh my God." I pressed a hand to my forehead, closing my eyes. "I'm so sorry for whatever he said, if it was unprofessional in any way—"

He waved me off. "It's forgotten. And, look, it's not my business who you date. Truth is, it's not anyone's business who you date, but I get the feeling that's not how things work here in Temperance Falls." He raised his eyebrows in question.

And really, what could I say? That was *exactly* how things worked on the island—part of the reason why I hadn't dated anyone in years. Why I'd wanted to keep things with Riley under the table.

"You're not wrong."

"I certainly don't expect you to be celibate. But any seemingly inconsequential incident could set off a former supporter—or tip a maybe-supporter back to the other side. I know you want this project here as much as I do. We don't need any added complications as we work together to get the vote, then the zoning permits for the mall."

"Of course. I want to make this transition as smooth as possible—for all parties involved."

"I appreciate that. I've enjoyed working with you, Kate. You're great at your job. But in a public position, the job isn't always what people notice, is it? I know that as well as anyone. If I were you, I'd keep things low-key between the two of you—at least until everything with this deal falls into place."

A knock sounded, and before I could respond to Colin, Riley poked his head around the door. "Hey, Lo wasn't out front, and I—" He broke off, straightening to his full height as soon as his eyes landed on the man across from me.

Colin looked at Riley, then turned back to me, eyebrows raised. With a quick rap of his knuckles on my desk, he stood to leave. "Thanks again for showing me around this afternoon." He walked to the door, nodding to Riley, then looked back at me. "And, Kate? Think about what I said."

Without another word, he slipped out the door, leaving Riley and me alone. I could only sit in silence, staring at where Colin had disappeared, his words turning over and over in my mind.

"What was that about?" Riley shut the door, then ate up the distance between us in two long strides.

I exhaled and closed my eyes, resting my elbows on my desk and my forehead in my hands. This was getting so damn complicated, and time had run out for me to figure out how the hell to handle it. Riley and I had an agreement, and yet here he was—in my office in the middle of the damn day. Tossing aside my requests as if they were meaningless. As if he weren't gambling with my career, with my *life*.

"What are you doing here?" I asked.

"I wanted to make sure you were okay after the tour."

"Riley…" I sighed.

"Don't be mad, Kitten." He ran a finger down the side of my face. "I took a stroll down the hall, and Lo was gone. I figured I could slip in and—"

"And interrupt my meeting with Colin." I dropped my hands and lifted my head. "Do you have any idea how bad this looked?"

"How bad what looked? That a fireman stopped in to see the mayor of the town he works in?" He clenched his jaw and stared out the window. With a quick shake of his head, he met my eyes again. "Look, I have to head to my parents' house for this dinner with Lola or my brother will castrate me. I know you said you didn't think it was a good idea, but why don't you come with me? They'd all be excited to meet you. Or if you don't want to deal with family stuff, we can head to Nonno Pino's for a bottle of wine and some cannoli."

I slapped my hand on my desk, my frustration getting the better of me. "Dammit, Riley, have you been listening to anything I've said?"

Snapping his jaw shut, he stepped back. Away from me. "Of course I have."

"If you have, you wouldn't keep *pushing*. I told you we need to take it slow, that we can't be seen on the island. And after your little show with Colin at the firehouse—"

"Colin? Are you kidding me with this right

now, Kate? What the fuck does he have to do with anything?"

"This is my job, Riley. My *career*. He has everything to do with it. He *knows*. And if he noticed something was going on between us, it's only a matter of time until other people do, too." I stood, fisting my hands at my sides. "I've worked too long, too hard for this. I can't just...I can't just give it up."

"I never asked you to give anything up. I'm pretty fucking sure I promised you the exact opposite, in fact." Running a hand through his hair, he walked in a circle, as if trying to get his emotions under control. "I've been patient. I've done what you've asked—taken you and fucked you in a run-down lighthouse where no one would see, when you deserved so much more. Just so I could be close to you. But this secret bullshit is really starting to wear on me. It's starting to wear on *us*."

"You knew at the beginning it wouldn't be forever. I'm not asking you to do this for the rest of your life, but I was very clear when you wanted to do this thing." I pointed my finger between the two of us. "That's why I didn't want to start anything in the first place. It's not fair for you to throw this back in my face now."

"Throw it in your face? I'm just trying to have a conversation with you." He groaned, closing his eyes as he scrubbed a hand down his face. "Look, I've got family stuff tonight. Why don't I go do that and just...leave you alone to figure out what you want? We could probably both use some time apart to think about things."

He circled my desk until he was close enough to grip my shoulders. Until he was close enough to envelop me in his familiar scent and warmth. He pressed his lips to my temple. "I *know* what I want, Kate. I thought I'd made that real fucking clear when I told you I love you. No deal to renovate an old mall or fear over one asshole member of the council is bigger than that…at least for me."

Of course it wasn't bigger than that for him. It was easy when it wasn't *his* career on the line…wasn't his livelihood, his life on the chopping block. Wasn't what he'd been working decades toward and didn't have to fight every damn day just to stay there.

"You need to figure out which is bigger to you." He strode out the door without a second glance, and I didn't do anything to stop him.

Didn't do anything but watch him leave.

chapter twelve

RILEY

TWENTY-FOUR HOURS ON an overtime shift after the conversation I'd had with Kate was about as torturous as I'd expected it to be. As much as I didn't want to wish a house fire on anyone—well, except maybe that asshole buying the mall—it would've been nice to have something to do to keep busy. Instead, I'd wallowed in a shitstorm of what-ifs, should-have-saids, and wish-I-hadn'ts.

When my shift at the firehouse finally ended, I honestly considered driving over to Kate's and demanding she talk to me. Not that I thought that was a good idea. She probably wasn't even there—it was a weekday. She was probably at her office, working away. Maybe in a meeting with that fucker who'd said something to put a wedge between us.

God, I couldn't go there. If I saw that jackass,

I'd beat the fuck out of him without thinking of the consequences. So I headed home alone instead. To my very empty, very Kateless apartment over the garage.

But when I turned into the driveway, a car I recognized as Kate's blocked my parking spot in front of the garage. My heart jumped and my stomach dropped all at once, hope and terror joining forces to make me feel sick. Especially when I saw Kate standing on the staircase right outside my door.

"What are you doing here?" I asked as soon as I stepped out of my car. I regretted my tone the second I caught her flinch. "Sorry. I just meant…you've never been here before. What's up?"

"I thought maybe we should talk."

Motherfucker. I knew those words, had heard men and women alike lament what came next when the person they were involved with said them. This was a breakup meeting, one I wasn't at all prepared for. One I wasn't ready to participate in. I needed to stall, to give myself time to figure out how to keep her from ending our relationship over what amounted to our first fight. I needed to keep her with me so I could convince her to give us another shot. That meant stonewalling her.

I grabbed my bag out of the trunk and headed up the stairs, refusing to give her even half a smile. "Talk about what?"

Kate fidgeted, looking unsure. Looking almost… scared. I'd never seen her like that. She wasn't a nervous woman—she was bold and confident, strong. Something was definitely wrong.

"Can we maybe go inside?" she asked, taking a deep breath and seeming to shore herself up. "I'd like to keep this private."

I loved the woman, but her need to keep everything fucking private was going to be the death of me. "Of course you would."

I unlocked the door and walked inside, leaving it open for Kate to follow. After tossing my bag down, I headed for my kitchenette. Might as well start drinking if I was about to have to fight to keep my girl.

"Want a beer?" I asked, knowing the answer she'd give before the question left my mouth.

She didn't disappoint. "It's only noon."

I grabbed a beer from the fridge, holding her gaze as I popped the cap off and took a swig. The beer was cold as it worked its way down my throat. Cold and bitter in a way I probably should have enjoyed. Instead, it burned what felt like a hole in my gut, and I set the bottle down on the counter after just the one drink.

Balls to the wall time.

"Well, you've got your privacy. What do you want to talk about?"

Kate looked around my apartment for a bit, moving with cautious footsteps toward the seating area. With a final sigh and a tug of her suit jacket, she took a seat on the black leather couch set along the wall. "How'd that thing with your parents go? Did they like Lola?"

"Of course they did. Lo's great, and Connor's

in love." I leaned against the counter, keeping my distance. Watching her like a hawk. Like a predator after his prey. "They'd love you, too, if you were willing to meet them."

Kate sighed, looking about as frustrated as I felt. "Riley…I know this has been difficult for you. Don't you think it's been hard for me, too?"

"I don't even know anymore, Kate. I was okay with the waiting, I really was. But that fucker put his hands on you at the firehouse. What did you expect me to do? Let him get away with that shit?"

"You're being ridiculous," she said, her voice growing louder. "Colin has only ever put his hands on me in a professional manner. He helped me up the stairs! Are you going to beat away every man who shakes my hand or holds open a door for me?"

"No, but if they drag you around like property, I'm certainly not going to stand by and do nothing. And you shouldn't take that shit from anyone."

"I've learned to pick and choose my battles. I've been in this world a long time. I know how to handle the men in it."

"And what about the men not in it? What about me, Kate? Have you figured out how to handle me yet?"

She took a deep breath and sagged into the couch, rubbing her fingers over her temples as if she had a headache. "This isn't going how I intended it to. I didn't want to start another fight. I just wanted to talk. About you. About us."

Every ounce of bravado dissipated. This was it. She was telling me goodbye. Time to man up and let her…so I could figure out how to stop this. "So talk. What is it you want to tell me?"

She licked her soft, full lips, a quick flick of her tongue against the pink I longed to steal one more taste of. Fuck, how could she still drive me mad and make me hard when things were so rocky between us? How could I ever let her walk away when she made me so—

"I love you," Kate said, completely derailing my self-pity party. She certainly had my attention. "Nothing's changed that. Not anything Colin said, not you acting like a caveman, not any of it. I love you, Riley."

There was no doubt in her words, no weakness in her body language. Confident Kate was back, telling me how she felt and meaning every syllable of it.

"I feel like there's a but coming after that statement, and not the kind I like to bite on."

The look she shot me could only be described as angry Kitten, claws and all. "*But* I'm scared. I'm scared about what us being together means for my life…for my career. I know I shouldn't care what other people think, but I have to—it comes with the territory of a public position. Especially one relying on those same people to vote for me to keep my job. And as much as I love you, my career means the world to me. I can't give it up—I *won't* give it up. Not even for you."

I stalked across the room, looming over Kate as she stood. "I don't remember asking you to give up anything."

Kate shook her head, looking up at me with those

blue eyes that seared my soul. "I know you like to pretend our age difference isn't there, but it is. *It is*, and that means I lived through a whole lot of heartbreak before you came along. I've already been here—I've been in relationships before where men pretended my job didn't matter, but it always ended the same way. They bailed when they realized I made twice as much as they did. When the hours added up and they started feeling neglected. When they realized I didn't need them in my life to feel fulfilled."

Aw, hell. That was what this was all about? Kate had blown something out of proportion, which was probably my fault. Still, this issue wasn't as dire as I'd thought. This was completely fixable.

"You think your job intimidates me?" I grabbed her by the ass, hauling her body up mine and heading for the bedroom. Fuck this fighting while clothed bullshit. If we were going to be getting to some make-up sex soon—and I was pretty sure we would be—I wanted us prepared for it. "You think I can't handle you being the mayor? The fact that you're a powerful woman is a fucking turn-on, Kitten. I'm not asking you to give up anything, not any part of your life as Mayor Kate Briscoe. I just want you to find a little room to let me be in it."

I tossed her onto the bed, crawling over her and pinning her in place. I needed to feel her, to experience that connection between us again. I needed to stoke the fire that always seemed to burn when we were together.

"I *do* want you in it." Kate spread her legs, giving

me room to lie between them as she ran her fingers down one side of my face. "I just…I've worked on this mall deal for three years, Riley. Three *years*. Nearly my entire term as mayor. And it all comes down to two weeks from now. If the council doesn't approve the rezoning, I fail."

I tugged her skirt up higher and moved her panties to the side, slipping my finger along her slit to tease her. She responded with a low moan, then worked her hands between us to push down my sweat pants. This was going to be quick and hot, I could already tell. But we weren't quite done talking. She still needed to know I had her back. Her front, her ass, her pussy…I had every part of her.

No fucking way was she failing on my watch.

"And you think I'm going to fuck things up for you? You think I can't understand the business you're in and help you?" I nudged two fingers inside her, rocking my hips against her thigh to get a little pressure on my cock. "I told you I'd be patient, and I was. But one, I won't let someone disrespect you. And two, we love each other. You deserve to be treated better than some random hookup, and I deserve not to have to live as your dirty little secret."

Kate grabbed my ass, groaning as I pushed my fingers in deep. "I know that. I *want* that. But Colin got antsy when he figured us out. He's spending almost a billion dollars on this project. Why did you have to say anything to him? Why couldn't you just let it go?"

I yanked her little shirt down, thankful she'd taken

off her suit jacket at some point. Fuck, her nipples were delicious. I had to bite on them a little, just enough to get her rocking against my hand. To get her slick and ready for my cock. "I would've helped you any way I could, but I'm not going to let other people disrespect you just to keep our love hidden. That's not my way, baby."

She groaned, arching her back and rubbing her clit against the side of my thumb. Greedy girl. "If this is gonna work, you have to trust that I can handle myself."

"Oh, baby. I know you can handle yourself. I've heard you do just that a few times over the last year."

Kate laughed and smacked my shoulder. "I'm being serious, Riley. I haven't gotten where I am by being soft." She punctuated the word soft with a solid grab of my very not-soft cock. The little tease. "You need to trust me to take care of my own shit."

I rocked into her hand, unable to hold still when her fingers felt so good on me. "Fine. But you need to trust that I can take care of your shit, too. You may not need me to, but I'm still going to be there, ready to take things off your plate when I see you overloaded. You also need to tell me exactly what's going on with you before I lose control and fuck you through the mattress. Goddamn, you have to stop jacking me off if you don't want me to come right now, Kitten."

She stopped, but she gave me that look—the one that said she needed to make sure I understood. The look of a woman saying something important. So

I pulled my hand from her pussy and stared down at her, ready for whatever was coming. Completely focused on her mouth.

"Tell me, Kate."

"I'm scared," she murmured, clinging to my arms and pulling me closer to her. "Men have never dealt well with my job, and I don't want it to be the same with you. I've never had this much to lose."

"Baby, the mall deal will go through. I'm sure of it."

She shook her head, lowering her voice as she said, "I'm not talking about the deal, Riley. I'm talking about you."

Everything inside me seemed to melt at once. My girl, my intelligent, capable woman, was afraid of losing me just as I'd been afraid of losing her. That totally made sense. It also made my heart want to do some fucking jumping jacks.

"Oh, Kitten, you're not losing me." I rolled us over, pulling her onto my chest as I settled on my back. "I've been over here plotting my way out of you breaking up with me, so no. I'm not going anywhere."

"You say that now, but other men—"

I yanked her down, refusing to let her say another word about other men. Those dicks were in the past. Kate's present, her future, was with me. And I'd make damn sure to keep it that way.

"If they can't handle a woman in charge, they're not men. Period." I grabbed her hips, rocking her sloppy, wet pussy all over my cock. "Now get up here and ride me, Ms. Mayor. I want to watch your tits bounce. We can figure out how to deal with Colin and the council after I've made you come two or six times."

"So bossy."

I reached for a condom from the nightstand with one hand and grabbed the back of her neck with the other, pulling her down for a deep kiss even as I placed the foil packet in her hand. "You like me that way."

"No," she said, giving me a true smile. "I love you that way."

"YOU HAVE GOT to be fucking kidding me."

"Riley, stop it." Kate pulled me into an exam room, giving me that look she sometimes did. The one that said I was super close to the line between protective and ridiculous. I bet if another woman were about to get up close and personal with my junk, she wouldn't think it so ridiculous.

She pushed me into a chair and closed the weird curtain that only blocked the door.

"This doesn't make any sense, though. Kitten, I want you to have the best doctor." I tried to sound calm, to stay serious and concerned, but my baby was stripping right there in front of me.

Her moves weren't specifically sexy—more utilitarian, really—but that didn't matter. Naked Kate was my favorite Kate, and she knew it. She'd worn a pretty, pink lace bra that made her tits irresistible, especially when she paired it with the expression she threw my way. That little glint in her eye was a tease meant just for me.

"You'd better quit looking at me that way, or I'm going to bend you over the exam table."

She hooked her thumbs in her panties—also pink, though not lacy—and dropped them to the floor. Fully fucking naked, and we were alone for at least another few minutes. I bet I could get a little taste if he—

"Is that before or after Dr. Caleb Goodman finishes his exam?"

Fuck. That took care of my erection. Slightly. "You're an evil woman." I made a point to adjust myself over my pants, staring right at her. If the flush of her chest was any indication, she got the message.

"Behave, Riley." As if I needed scolding.

"How can I when you're this beautiful? It's impossible." I definitely earned that flush. Good, because I wasn't done with the whole doctor thing yet. "But seriously, baby. How can this guy be the best on the island? Shouldn't a doctor with the same equipment as the patient be the best?"

She rolled her eyes and pulled one of those paper sheet things around her, covering her nakedness. Not even close to good enough when there was about to be another man in this room, but I was pretty sure she wasn't budging on this whole thing.

"Dr. Goodman is the best Maternal-Fetal Medicine specialist in the state, and he just happens to live on the island. We should consider ourselves lucky."

"I need to run for the school board," I said, not at all happy even though I'd been right—she wasn't budging. "Need to get some girls into those STEM classes and stuff. Start 'em in science young so they become the experts on all things…woman."

Kate just laughed. "You're ridiculous. Adorable, but ridiculous."

I wasn't going to argue with her, especially not when she was looking up at me the way she was. I couldn't resist those soft, sweet smiles of hers. I tugged her closer, running my thumb over the ring on her finger. The one I'd put there just the week before in front of a handful of friends and family. The one that said she was mine.

"Not ridiculous, just lucky as sin and so fucking grateful."

"I am, too, you know," she whispered, holding the side of my face. "Lucky and grateful."

I let that statement lie, even though I could've argued for days about how I was the lucky one. She was my heart, my soul—the one woman who could calm the storm in my mind and draw me back to my hometown. She was it for me, and I'd do everything I could to make sure I earned her heart.

When she was ready, I helped Kate onto the exam table. She probably could've done it herself, but why would I let her? She was in a fragile state, something she'd deny in a heartbeat if I tried to point that out. But seriously, the woman was carrying my baby. A baby neither of us had planned on or tried for. A fucking miracle considering Kate had been on birth control and we'd used condoms that whole first month together. My boys were unstoppable…a statement I could never say to Kate without getting The Look.

The door opened just as someone knocked twice, and a man's voice asked, "Everyone ready for me?"

"No," I whispered into Kate's ear, making her giggle.

"Yes, of course." Kate grabbed my hand as the curtain blocking the door opened wide and a tall man with glasses walked in. What was this…Doogie Howser? He looked younger than me. "How are you, Dr. Goodman?"

The so-called doctor typed a few things into the tablet he held before smiling at Kate. "I'm good, but the question of the hour is how are you, Madam Mayor? Adjusting to this new adventure okay?"

I huffed a laugh, and Kate hit my arm. "I'm fine. Adjusting to the idea of…a baby."

Her smile nearly knocked me out, and I simply had to lean down to kiss her forehead. Yeah, she was adjusting. It'd been a rough couple of weeks after she'd found out she was pregnant. I wouldn't ever forget the look of abject panic on her face when she'd come racing into the firehouse to tell me. She hadn't been able to hold back her words, had stumbled over half-formed sentences and rambled on about all the things that could go wrong before she finally looked right at me and blurted out, "I'm pregnant."

Thankfully, only Big John had been in the truck

bay when she'd said that. Otherwise, the whole fucking island would know. We weren't ready for that. John had told me to take my girl home, that he'd get someone to cover for me. A fact I still owed him for. Kate and I'd hunkered down at her place for two days, going back and forth about what this meant and how things would change.

All the while, I'd waited for her to wrap her head around the fact that we'd made a baby so we could celebrate the shit out of that. My Kitten needed to process stuff, though. She needed to get her bearings. It took time. Thank fuck I was a patient man.

"Why don't you lie back and put your feet in the stirrups, Kate?" Dr. Goodman typed a little more in his tablet before setting it on the counter behind him and taking far too long to wash his hands. Finally, he took the seat next to Kate's bed. The one with the computer set up in front of it. "Your blood work all looks great. We're just going to do an internal ultrasound to better estimate the age of the fetus. I'm sure you're aware, but with your age—"

"Yeah." My girl sounded pissed as fuck. "I know. I'm too old to have a baby."

"Not at all." Goodman smiled as he placed something that looked like Bob Barker's microphone from *The Price is Right* between Kate's spread knees. What the fuck was that? "You're perfectly healthy and obviously able to have a baby. We just like to keep a closer eye on things when our mothers are a bit more experienced at life."

"See, Kate," I said, leaning over her. "You're not

too old to be a mom. You're just more experienced at life."

"I will rip your dick off if you ever say that to me again."

I cocked a grin and leaned down to whisper in her ear. "But then you'd be back to silicone and batteries, baby. We both know that's not enough for you anymore."

Kate tried to throw me a wicked sort of glare, but her lips twitched as if she were fighting a smile. "Cut it out, Riley."

"Yes, ma'am."

"Okay," the doctor said, moving his arm around to where it disappeared under Kate's gown. He had his hand on her pussy. On my pussy. That was all I could think about. At least until he started pointing a little red light toward the television at the end of the bed. "This is the placenta, and this is all amniotic fluid. Everything looks good, nice proportions." He clicked a few buttons, and the picture zoomed in on a white blob. "And this is your baby."

I stared as he froze the picture and used something to take measurements. Nothing he said mattered anymore. That was my baby. Our baby. When Kate had said she was pregnant, I'd believed her, but this... this was real. This was... My fucking baby was on that screen. Even if it did just look like a tiny white...blob.

A thumping sort of buzzing suddenly filled the room, and I tore my eyes away from my baby to check on the doctor. He focused on the screen, his arm still between Kate's legs.

"There we go," he said, grinning at Kate and me. "That's your baby's heartbeat."

Kate's hand squeezed mine, and when I looked down, she was staring at the screen with the most beautiful smile I'd ever seen. We locked gazes as the sound of our baby's life filled the room, as it beat so fucking fast. How could it beat so fast?

"It's quick," Kate whispered, echoing my thoughts. The tone of her voice, the happiness and relief I heard there, was too much.

"It's beautiful." I leaned down to kiss her, my heart about to burst. "You're beautiful."

The sound continued for several minutes as the doctor babbled on about size and measurements, but I didn't care. I had everything I ever could have wanted and more than I'd ever dreamed of having right there in my arms. He was no longer a concern.

"And that's about it," Dr. Goodman said eventually. The sound of my future cut off without warning, and he removed his hand from between Kate's legs.

The doctor stood and tossed his gloves in the trash before heading to the sink to wash his hands. "Everything looks great. You're in excellent health, and the baby is progressing just as it should. Take your vitamins, drink your water, and try not to work yourself to death. You're still going to be a little tired and likely sick to your stomach at times. Carry snacks with you, or the front desk has sour and ginger candies that may help. Do you have any questions for me?"

Kate glanced my way, turning back to the doc

once I shook my head. I'd already read that *What to Expect When You're Expecting* book and about six others I'd found at the local bookstore. I had a good understanding of the basics.

"No, I think we're good," she said.

"Great. Then I'll let you two get back to your day." He typed a few things into his tablet as he headed for the door. "I want you back in one month, Kate. I need to take extra good care of the mayor's baby."

With that, he was gone, and I was staring down at my entire world. "The mayor's baby."

"I heard." Her smile fell, and she had that look on her face like she thought I wasn't going to like what she had to say. "Riley, are you sure about this? I mean, it's so—"

I kissed her hard and deep, stopping her words. We'd been around this merry-go-round a hundred times since she came bursting into the firehouse looking like she'd seen a ghost and babbling about babies and being selfish and...

Well, a bunch of bullshit, really.

"I've got this," I whispered, going back for a few more soft kisses before holding her face in my hands and resting my forehead against hers. "Remember when I promised you that your career would be safe with me? I meant it. We're having a baby, and once we do, you're going to do whatever you want. Right now, that's go back to work and run again in the next election. That's fine by me."

She grabbed my wrists, her eyes looking

suspiciously watery. "I don't know if I can handle letting strangers watch our baby."

Oof. Yeah, that wasn't happening. "Kitten, we were both raised here. We know just about every fucking person on this island. They wouldn't be strangers."

"Riley—"

"I'll take a leave of absence." I grinned when she jerked back, the idea something I hadn't given much thought to but one that felt right. "I'll stay home with the baby while you work. I can pick up a few construction jobs with Jackson along the way to keep making money, but we'll schedule them when you or my mom or, hell, even my brother can watch the baby. It's not a problem."

She was giving me The Look again. "You'd give up your career?"

"I'd go back once the baby went to school."

"Riley, that's five years."

"So?"

"So…five years is a lifetime."

I pulled her into my arms, holding her tight and rocking her. "Five years is a blink, it's nothing. And we'll be together the whole time, which is all that's important. What more could I want?"

"You're crazy."

"No, I'm trying to take care of you. You want to go back to work? Awesome. Don't want to hire a nanny, though? That means I need to step up. I'll quit my job and get all Mr. Mom up in the place. Easy." I rolled my eyes and gave her one more smacking kiss when she still wouldn't relax. "You go change the world, Kitten. I'll change the diapers."

The way she bit her lip had me wishing we were someplace where I could take advantage of her still-naked state. I tugged up the back of her paper gown and ran my hand over her hip, needing to feel her. Wanting to touch.

Kate leaned into me, her breasts pressing against my chest. "What will people say when you tell them you're staying home with the baby?"

"They'd better say what an amazing father I am and how lucky I must be to have such a strong and successful partner." I twirled the ring she wore. The one that tied her to me. "How lucky my wife is that she's married to such a progressive guy."

"I am, you know. So lucky."

"I know, but it goes both ways." I gave her ass a pat—how could I not?—then handed her the clothes she'd set on the chair beside me. "As much as it pains me to say it, let's get you dressed and back to work. You've got a groundbreaking ceremony to get to."

The frown she sent me was a good one. "Ugh, don't remind me."

Watching her slide her clothes on was almost as sexy as watching her take them off. The way the cotton and lace slipped into place, how she bent and turned to make sure everything lay just right. I could watch her put on clothes every day for the rest of our lives. And I would—though I'd also be watching her take them off. That was for sure. "You can skip it, you know."

She patted her hair into place and grabbed her bag. "It's the mall project. I can't skip. This is the biggest deal of my career."

I dropped my hand to her belly as she tried to move past me, stopping her. "For now."

The smile she gave me lit up her face like nothing else, and her fingers were warm as they weaved with mine. "For now."

We walked out of the office and headed for the car, me keeping Kate close to my side. I drove, holding her hand the entire way, too keyed up about her and the baby to give her the option. Thank God she understood my protectiveness. Understood it and definitely seemed to welcome it at this stage.

The drive to the mall took no time at all, and Kate was in pure business mode when we arrived. Reading over lists, checking her phone…absorbed by the logistics of the whole thing.

"Thirty minutes," I said as I helped her out of the car. "We're in for thirty minutes, then we're going home."

"Fine. Your fan club is here." She nodded to the group of women standing at one side of the stage. Yeah, her events tended to be real fucking popular with that crowd. Popular because of me. Not that I paid any attention to them other than to be polite.

"So is yours." I kissed her, squeezing a handful of ass to make my point. "Thirty minutes and we're going home so you can rest."

"You're being ridiculous."

"You threw up three times this morning."

"I have work to do, Riley."

With Kate, you had to pick your battles, and this wasn't one I was going to win. "Fine. But I'm getting you some fucking crackers and a water."

She rose up to give me a kiss, mumbling something about silly and sweet before heading for the stage. It was time for her show, for her moment. And I was more than happy to let her shine. She had my ring on her finger and my baby in her belly. What more could I ask for?

"Everything okay over here?" Big John slipped in beside me, staring at the stage just as I'd been.

"What are you doing here, man?"

John shrugged, his eyes still on the stage. Or rather, one particular person on that stage. "Same thing you are, I suppose."

Emery chatted with Kate, the two women oblivious to the men in the audience tracking their every move. Not all men, just me…and John.

I kept my voice down, leaning into John's side. "You and Emery?"

John grunted. He slapped one big hand on my shoulder, harder than he needed to. Making a point, it seemed. "See you at work."

I nodded once, grinning. "Sure will. We can have a chat."

"Fuck your chat." He stormed off as I laughed. Kate must have heard me because she turned, meeting my eyes for a moment before grinning. Emery turned as well, frowning after John's retreating figure. Those two would have to work out their own stuff, though.

My wife held one hundred percent of my attention. Especially as she stepped in front of the podium, her mayoral smile in place.

"Friends and neighbors, we're here to kick off a construction project three years in the making."

As Kate spoke about partnerships and moving the island's economy forward, I stood and watched her shine. This was her talent, her skill—she was an awesome speaker and a thoughtful leader. Most of the residents of the island loved her. Just not as much as I did.

As I had since the first time her voice had come over my phone.

As I would for the rest of my life.

also available from
TEMPERANCE FALLS
Reunion
LONDON HALE

She's ready to move on

High school reunions are supposed to be fun. Unfortunately, mine starts with a storm that traps me in a house with my newly ex-boyfriend...and his hot-as-sin stepbrother. Luke kept in touch with me over the years, but not like this. Not with his hands, his fingers... his mouth. If my ex finds out, it's more than just a friendship on the line. I could destroy a family.

He's done holding back

Hannah's been off limits for twelve long years, ever since my stepbrother swooped in and claimed her before I could. As if coveting from afar isn't bad enough, now I have to suffer through our ten year reunion watching them together. But things aren't as perfect in paradise as it would seem. One overheard conversation between them, and I'm ready to throw caution to the wind. If my stepbrother can't make her scream, I'm more than happy to get the job done.

about the author

London Hale is the combined pen name of writing besties Ellis Leigh and Brighton Walsh. Between them, they've published more than thirty books in the contemporary romance, paranormal romance, and romantic suspense genres. Ellis is a *USA Today* bestselling author who loves coffee, thinks green Skittles are the best, and prefers to stay in every weekend. Brighton is multi-published with Berkley, St. Martin's Press, and Carina Press. She hates coffee, thinks green Skittles are the work of the devil, and has never heard of a party she didn't want to attend. Don't ask how they became such good friends or work so well together—they still haven't figured it out themselves.

www.londonhale.com